The Heart of a Savage 3

Jibril Williams

**Lock Down Publications and Ca$h
Presents**
The Heart of a Savage 3
A Novel by *Jibril Williams*

The Heart of a Savage 3

Lock Down Publications
P.O. Box 944
Stockbridge, Ga 30281

Visit our website @
www.lockdownpublications.com

Copyright 2021 Jibril Williams
The Heart of a Savage 3

This is a work of fiction. Names, characters, places, and incidents either are products of the author's imagination or are used fictitiously. Any similarity to actual events or locales or persons, living or dead, is entirely coincidental.

Lock Down Publications
Like our page on Facebook: Lock Down Publications @
www.facebook.com/lockdownpublications.ldp
Cover design and layout by: **Dynasty Cover Me**
Book interior design by: **Shawn Walker**
Edited by: **Jill Alicea**

Jibril Williams

Stay Connected with Us!

Text **LOCKDOWN** to 22828 to stay up-to-date with
new releases, sneak peaks, contests and more…
Thank you.

Submission Guidelines

Submit the first three chapters of your completed manuscript to ldpsubmissions@gmail.com, subject line: Your book's title. The manuscript must be in a .doc file and sent as an attachment. Document should be in Times New Roman, double spaced and in size 12 font. Also, provide your synopsis and full contact information. If sending multiple submissions, they must each be in a separate email.

Have a story but no way to send it electronically? You can still submit to LDP/Ca$h Presents. Send in the first three chapters, written or typed, of your completed manuscript to:

LDP: Submissions Dept
P.O. Box 944
Stockbridge, Ga 30281

DO NOT send original manuscript. Must be a duplicate.

Provide your synopsis and a cover letter containing your full contact information.

Thanks for considering LDP and Ca$h Presents.

Jibril Williams

Chapter 1

"Oh God, grant me the serenity to accept the things I cannot change. Grant me the courage to change the things I can, and the wisdom to know the difference between my friends and my foes. Grant my husband forgiveness for all his transgressions, and accept him into your kingdom. Bestow upon me your mercy as I commit these heinous acts. I know you have the power to forgive, but I don't."

Jelli rose off her bended knees from prayer. She wiped her tears away with the palms of her hands. Today she was scheduled to lay her fiancé to rest. *Whoever said that 'every day that goes by after losing someone gets better'—They are a muthafuckin liar,* Jelli thought to herself. *The bitter truth is that it hurts just as bad today, just as it did nine days ago.* Jelli walked over to her king-size bed that she used to share with Cain, and removed his pillow. She buried her face into the pillow and inhaled deeply, trying to catch the natural scent of Cain. His scent will be embedded in her mind until God stops her broken heart.

Jelli closed her eyes, and her mind immediately went back to the night her fiancé was murdered. "Over here! You got someone shot over here, he's still alive!" Jelli called out, frantically waving her arms in the air, trying to get the attention of the paramedics that just arrived at the crime scene—Club Bass & Cru parking lot. The paramedics were followed by a fleet of DC Metropolitan police cruisers. The medics jumped out the ambulance, and quickly assisted Cain who was bleeding from gunshot wounds. "Sir, what's your name?" the chief medic asked, checking Cain's vitals.

"Cain—Cain Ross," Cain stated, floating in and out of consciousness. The medics immediately loaded Cain into the back of the ambulance after packing his wounds with gauzes, and started him on an IV.

Jelli tried to climb aboard the ambulance with Cain and the paramedics. "I'm sorry, ma'am, but you can't ride in the rig with us—only immediate family." Jelli wanted to scream at the slightly obese medic. *Fucker, are you serious! This is my fuckin' fiancé; he just proposed to me*, Jelli thought to herself. So, to avoid argument, and out of a deep concern to get her fiancé to the hospital, Jelli shot daggers with her eyes, as she descended off the back of the ambulance.

"Okay, I'll follow you there!" Jelli said quickly, turning on her heels and making her way to Cain's Bentley Bentayga. She hopped in the luxury vehicle and sped off behind the ambulance, racing through traffic. The ambulance sirens blared all the way, notifying the traffic ahead of them that there was an emergency and they needed to pull over and clear the way.

A few impatient drivers shot right back into traffic, once the ambulance passed them. A driver of a red Toyota Highlander, and a green Honda, had cut Jelli off. She had to double tap her brakes to avoid T-boning the Honda. Jelli let her thumb ride the horn button on the Bentayga steering wheel, letting the drivers ahead of her know they were in error. "Bitch, what the fuck!" Jelli yelled.

A black Tahoe out of nowhere cut the ambulance off. The rig skidded to a halt, barely missing the Tahoe. The two cars behind the ambulance had it boxed in. Jelli watched as a masked woman sprung from the passenger side of the Tahoe. Holding a bronze colored Mack 10, the masked woman rushed to the rear of the ambulance. Jelli watched in horror, as the masked woman forced the medics out the back of the ambulance with gunfire. "No!" Jelli yelled out, watching behind two cars. When Jelli heard the cracking of the shooter's gun, she knew she had lost Cain forever.

Yanking that tragic experience out of her mind, Jelli opened her eyes, and pulled the pillow away from her face, planting Cain's scent deep inside her memory. She placed the pillow back in the bed, and the floodgates of tears and pain were open. There was nothing that Jelli could do but let the faucet of her tears run free like a river until she could cry no more.

Every time Jelli closed her eyes for any period of time, the murder of her fiancé would revisit her so vividly like a bright moon on a dark night. Tears of love and hate washed over her face over the past year. Cain had become her loving knight. He sheltered her with love that's constantly read about in books and viewed in them chick flicks that so many hood niggas dread to watch with their so-called love of their lives. Cain made Jelli feel accomplished in the way that he loved her. It boosted her confidence, and had her feeling like she was flawless even though she knew she had many defects. Jelli didn't know how she was going to live without Cain. However, since his death, a new strength kindled within her. That strength could only be obtained through hate and revenge. This new vitality in Jelli wouldn't allow her to just walk away; if she did, Cain's love was all for nothing. Tata and the Red Bottom Squad have to pay for what they'd done to Cain. They didn't have to kill her fiancé, or violate their sisterhood the way they did. Tata jumped the gun on the situation. Tata didn't give her a chance to hash shit out with Cain about Phatmama killing Cain's cousin—Rocco. It would have been a hard task to convince Cain to forgive her girls for his cousin's death, but there was no way Phatmama couldn't have known who Rocco was, or who he was affiliated with. In Jelli's mind there was no doubt Cain would have spared her girls for her because he loved her just that damn much. A knock at the door interrupted Jelli's crying session "Yeah!" Jelli answered.

"The car is ready," Fate said through the bedroom door.

"I'll be down in a minute!" Jelli yelled back through the door. Walking over to the vanity, Jelli checked her puffy eyes in the mirror. She brushed the wrinkles out her black Fendi shirt, clipping the leather side hustler on her side. She grabbed the matching Fendi suit jacket off the back of the chair in front of the vanity. She stared in the mirror at herself one last time before she placed the dark Fendi shades on her face. She was ready to go bury her husband and bring hell on earth to the Red Bottom Squad.

Thirty minutes later, Jelli arrived at the funeral home. The parking lot was packed with Cain's loved ones and luxury whips. Fate climbed from behind the wheel of Jelli's Lexus RX 450h, and made his way to the passenger side's back door. He looked around briefly before opening the truck's door. Jelli paused for a few seconds, and made eye contact with Fate through her dark Fendi glasses. Fate could sense Jelli's hesitation, as he extended his calloused hand to her. She waved his hand off. She didn't want to seem weak in front of so many spectators. Jelli's black four-inch Giuseppe Stilettos met the pavement, and she pulled herself from the SUV. The security team swooped in, and escorted her into the funeral home. Then everyone in the parking lot followed behind Jelli into the funeral home to pay their last respect.

On the way in, Jelli and Fate were met by Diego. The glare in his eyes explained the pain he was experiencing in his heart. The fire in his eyes also told the story that Diego was trying to mask the death of his uncle—Cain—with drug use. Lost in his thoughts, Diego slightly bumped against

Jelli as he walked by. Fate placed a vice-grip hand on his arm and pulled Diego close to him. The black jeans and hoodie let Fate know Diego was in kill mode. Fate whispered in his ear: "Be at the meeting tomorrow. I'm on go mode too, but first let's bury your uncle. Don't go out and do nothing stupid."

Diego's nostrils flared. He yanked away from Fate's grip and kept it mobbin. Fate was about to go after him. But Jelli shook her head, indicating that Fate should let Diego be.

Jelli made her way down towards the front of the funeral home, where a pearly white coffin with black and gray swirl marble trimmings and handles rested, encased with multiple arrays of flowers. There were so many flowers, Jelli couldn't even count them all. Jelli finally made it to Cain's casket. She refused to have a close casket service. Now, after seeing Cain's head covered in black net, her knees buckled. Fate and another body guard had caught her before she could make contact with the floor. Fate steadied Jelli. "You're alright? You can get through this," Fate whispered.

Jelli didn't convey any words verbally, but she nodded, confirming that she was okay. She steadied herself on Cain's casket. She placed a hand over her mouth with a trembling hand. The floodgate from this morning was once again open, and the tears were relentless. Jelli leaned over into Cain's casket and planted kisses on his face. "I love you, baby—I will never forget your love, our love—I miss you so much," Jelli whispered in the ear of her fiancé's corpse.

The mourners stood back at the first pew. They waited patiently for Jelli to say her goodbye. Jelli couldn't let them see Cain in this horrible state. The net over his head was just too much. She wanted the people to remember Cain's smiling face, not him laid in a casket with a net over his head. She fished her smartphone out of her Fendi bag, and pulled up a picture of Cain smiling and full of life. Jelli eased the top down on Cain's casket and propped her smartphone up on its lid, displaying and broadcasting the handsome face of Cain "There you go, baby," Jelli mumbled as she placed a manicured hand on Cain's casket. "The war begins now," Jelli whispered, walking away and taking a seat in the first pew.

Chapter 2

The Other Side of Town

The Red Bottom Squad sat stone-faced in the front row of Shallow Baptist Church. Zoey's grandmother—Ms. Hanna—sat next to Tata, crying her heart out over a slain Zoey. She squeezed Tata's hand tightly. Every time Ms. Hanna would mumble the words "My baby", a river of tears would slide from under the dark Versace shades Tata tried to hide behind. She didn't want the world to see her pain. Tata rubbed the back of Ms. Hanna's hand as she held hers.

The Red Bottom Squad was sending one of their very own out in style. The budget for the funeral was unlimited. Zoey rested comfortably in a gray casket with pink trimmings. The colors were Zoey's favorite. The white Versace dress fitted firmly on her body, as she laid there with a pair of Versace shoes gracing her feet. Tata had a professional make-up artist come in and do Zoey's make-up. It didn't even look like Zoey had passed over to the afterlife. It looked as though she was laying down resting briefly before she went out to the club.

Zoey's hair was down. A gold princess crown adorned her head, and a black diamond sat at its centerpiece—One of the nine black diamonds the squad heisted from a job they pulled off months ago. Zoey was ready to be sent home to her Lord. The preacher was putting a closure to his sermon. Tata didn't hear a word of it. She was deep in her thoughts of murder. *Cain's organization must perish for this— There's no question about this*, Tata thought to herself. The team had agreed that they would bury Zoey first before they turn up the heat on Cain's people. Tata thought since Cain was the head of his crime family, his organization would

13

wither and die after his death, but she'd been getting reports from Whip and Boot that Cain's organization was still up and running. She wondered whether Diego or Cain's body-guard—Fate— had claimed the throne. It didn't really matter; they both were already marked for death—including Jelli.

It would have taken Tata a million years to be convinced that Jelli would side with Cain the way she did. Tata was convinced that Jelli had told Cain about Phatmama killing his cousin Rocco. There was no reason why Cain would come out the club with his men gunning for them. Considering all the shit they had been through together: prison yard fights, robbing jewelry stores, to murdering muthafuckas, Tata couldn't believe Jelli's actions. *It was supposed to be family over niggas.* Tata shook her head at the thought of Jelli's treason. She wiped away some of the tears that trickled down her face. Tata glanced over to Phatmama who was sitting next to her. Phatmama's leg rapidly bounced up and down, indicating she was about to spaz out. Phatmama loved Zoey like a true sister. *A river of blood will fill the cracks of D.C. streets behind the death of Zoey,* Phatmama swore deep inside her. Phatmama was going to make sure of that. She was feeling like it was her fault that Zoey was lying in that box, and she was determined to unleash her wrath on Jelli after Zoey was laid to rest.

Tata reached over and placed a hand on Phatmama's knee, bringing her bouncing knee to a halt. She squeezed it, giving Phatmama the reassurance that she was feeling the pain of losing Zoey. Tata looked at her right on the other side, where she saw a weeping Ms. Hanna seated with her head down, tears dropping on the top of the bereaved woman's hands. Tata twirled a Chiappa Rhino .375 bullet between her fingers. It was odd how quickly Zoey and Racks grown so close.

"My baby!" Ms. Hanna yelled out. Tata wrapped her arms around Ms. Hanna, and placed her head against hers, rocking back and forth with the elderly woman.

"Be strong for her, Ms. Hanna," Tata whispered. Finally, the preacher finished with his sermon. The church stood to view Zoey's body one last time. After each person went up for their final view, they exited the church and waited for Zoey's casket to be brought out of the church. The church held about a hundred attenders—Many of the people Tata didn't know, but they knew Zoey through her golden glove days. Tata made her way out the church, and stood next to Whip at the bottom of the steps of the church. Whip was a straight up hood nigga, and he didn't do churches at all. But, on the strength of Tata, he held the fort down from outside with his trusted comrade—Boot—beside him. He leaned over, kissed Tata on the cheek, and whispered in her ear: "Everything a go. Just waiting on you to green-light it."

Tata nodded. Ms. Hanna was still glued to her side, and she didn't want to say anything to alarm the sixty-five-year old woman. So she mouthed the word, "Wait!" to Whip. Boot eased next to Phatmama and entwined his fingers into hers. Since the night he helped Phatmama smash Cain, a sick type of bond was ignited between the two.

The six pallbearers came out of the church with Zoey's casket hoisted on their shoulders. The onlookers watched in silence. You could hear a sweet melody being sung by a chocolate heavy-set woman who sang her heart out about going home to Jesus, as she marched behind the pallbearers. A light breeze brushed against Tata's cheek. She felt like it was a sign that Zoey was telling her she was okay. The pall-bearers reached the waiting hearse. They lowered Zoey's casket into the back of it. Family and friends began to load into their own individual cars so that could follow the hearse to the grave site.

A few family members piled into the waiting limousine. Tata escorted Ms. Hanna to the limousine. "No, child, I want to ride with you.

Tata didn't have a problem with Ms. Hanna's request. "Sure, Ms. Hanna," Tata stated with her arm around Ms. Hanna. Whip was waiting at Tata's G37 Infiniti truck. He helped Ms. Hanna in the back seat after she refused to sit up front. Tata climbed in and buckled her seatbelt. The hearse eased into traffic; the limousine followed behind it, and Whip jumped behind the limousine.

Tata laid her head back on the head rest, thinking of her next move. The concession line turned on Rhode Island Ave. Two black Bronco trucks came off a side street. One cut in front of the hearse, and the other barraged its way in between the limousine and the back of the hearse. The limousine slammed on the brakes, causing Whip to hit his brakes. The front Bronco slowed and stopped, causing the funeral line to be held up in traffic. Tata rose in her seat, trying to see what the fuck was going on. Four groups of niggas wearing ghost masks, like the one worn in the movie 'Scream', stormed out of the front Bronco. They were gripping AR-15's and wearing Rest in Peace Cain shirts. They rushed to the back of the hearse, and pulled Zoey's casket from the back of the hearse. The coffin hit the ground with a loud thump. Ms. Hanna screamed out, "My baby!"

"Listen to me, Ms. Hanna, lay down on the floor and don't get up until I tell you," Tata said, as she reached in her glove compartment and removed her Glock. Ms. Hanna followed Tata's orders and got on the floor of Tata's truck and began to pray. Whip checked his mirrors; he saw Phatmama and Boot bailing out, Boots Whip sprinting his way. Zoey's casket lay in the middle of the street. One of the gunmen shot the locks off Zoey's casket, opening it. Tata and Whip tried to get out the truck to defend, but the shooters' AR's lit up and sent about a dozen shots their way. The shooters' bullets ate into Tata's truck. They couldn't return fire, so they got low in the truck. They could hear shots popping off from a distance. Whip knew that was Boot and Phatmama trying to get the shooters off them. The gunmen let off more shots, trying to air Phatmama and Boot out. *Boom!* A shot rang out, and one of the shooter's head exploded.

One of the masked men hooked Zoey's legs up to some type of cord, and attached it to the back of the Bronco. The shooters hopped back in the trucks, and cleared it, dragging Zoey's body with them. The way Zoey's body rolled and bounced on the pavement as it was dragged wasn't something a sane person could fathom. Ms. Hannah yelled: "My baby!" Her yell was eardrum-shattering. Tata grabbed Whip by his arm. "Green-light that shit now!"

Whip fumbled with his phone as he sent the message.

***

The hearse Jelli followed behind got caught at a red light at a four-way intersection. She had a long morning. She sent her fiancé out in style. They were now headed to the graveyard to lay Cain to rest. Three stolen Dodge Magnums pulled up on the side of the hearse—two on the right, one on the left. Fate thought it was odd for three cars of the same make and model to be in the same place at the same time.

The tint on the Magnums was so dark, you couldn't see the inside of the cars.

The light turned green, and one of the Magnums hit it and jumped in front of the hearse, stopping the funeral line from proceeding. The doors opened on the opposite side of the hearse. Fate knew it was a hit. Shooters hopped out the Dodges with red bandanas tied around their faces. They open fire on Fate and Jelli with Mack 10s.

Yak-yak-yak-yak!

Fate threw the SUV in reverse, ramming into the car of his security detail. The wind shield dropped on top of his head, a bullet found its way through his hand. "Fuck!" Fate yelled.

The shooters continued shooting up at Fate. Then they sent a hail of bullets into the hearse, shattering its window, exposing Cain's coffin that rested in its cabin. The shooters lit bottles filled with gas, and rags hanging out their openings, and threw them inside the hearse with Cain's casket.

Swooosh! A roaring blaze started. The shooters threw up the blood signs, jumped back into their stolen cars, and pulled out, leaving Cain's body to burn to a crisp.

Chapter 3

"Diego, what the fuck was that shit you pulled yesterday? That shit was reckless!" Fate yelled. The youngsta respected Fate, but he wasn't a bitch, and he wasn't gonna let Fate treat him as such.

"Bruh, chill with the high volume in your voice. I'm not trying to hear that shit you barking. My fuckin' uncle was murdered by some hoe ass bitches, and you all muthafuckas sitting around twirling ya muthafuckin thumbs, worrying about all the wrong shit." There was a distinct edge to Diego's voice. He was getting heated. His chest rose and fell with adrenaline. Diego was on a hurt mission.

Fate could see the rage in the boy's eyes. And the savage shit he pulled yesterday at Zoey's funeral told the level of his savageness. The killing of his uncle had activated that beast within him. This new aspect of Diego could be a great asset to the Cain crime family, if it could be harnessed right.

"Diego, trust me, every muthafucka and every scandalous bitch that had something to do with your uncle's death will feel the wrath of this family. But first, we must secure the plug. Without the plug, we don't continue to eat. Cain would roll over in his grave—" Fate paused, thinking about the burning hearse Cain laid blazed in. At that moment, Fate's hand started to ache where one of the shooter's bullets drilled a hole in it. "What I'm trying to say is that everything Cain worked so hard for will cease to exist if we don't secure the plug."

Fate damn near raised Diego right along with Cain. But Diego felt Fate was acting nonchalant about Cain's death. He understood clearly what Fate was saying about securing the connect, and not letting his uncle's legacy die in vain. The C.C.F (Cain Crime Family) must live on, by any means.

But Fate could have shown some emotion about his boss's death. And that's what alarmed Diego.

"I hear ya, Fate, and that's why I'm here at this meeting to continue to carry my uncle's torch," Diego said. It just occurred to him that he was not in line to sit at the head of the table of the CCF Empire. At that instant, so many thoughts riffled through his mind. He needed to sit down and process the realization of the present situation. All at once, Diego balled his face up. "Hold up, hold the fuck up! Who been running the business since unc' been dead? Who been collecting all the bread from the traps, and where that paper at?" Diego said aggressively.

"It's about time you open your fuckin' eyes and started thinking outside of your anger!" Fate retorted, not answering Diego's questions." It's some shit goin' on. I went to the main stash spots and the two hundred bricks are missing. All of the last shipment is gone. I went to your uncle's duck off crib out Lorton VA. Everything was intact but the walk-in safe was empty." Fate finished his words with a crease in his forehead.

"Who else knew about my uncle's spots other than you and me?" Diego's hand rested on the handle of his Taurus 45. that was under his black "Rest in Peace" Cain shirt. Fate felt slightly offended from Diego's hand movement. However, with what was at stake, he understood.

"Diego, I don't know who else knew about them spots other than me and you, but the way the house was left undamaged, someone had keys and access code to get in the house and the safe."

"So you fuckin' telling me that you knew my uncle's product and money just up and vanish without a trace and you haven't said shit? I see a muthafuckin snake in the grass, Fate, and if you don't start making sense out of this situation, I'm about to chop the snake's head off." Diego spoke through clenched teeth, as he pulled the .45 off his hip.

A glimpse of panic appeared in Fate's eyes, but it disappeared almost immediately. "I worked for your uncle for over twelve years, and I never stole a dime. Every dime was turned in. I watched his back out there in them cold streets so your little ass could lay in a warm bed at night, and now you stand in front of me with your chest up, with your gun out, accusing me of being a snake, a disloyal muthafucka! If you think that my character is that flawed, then put a bullet in my head and drag my body through the streets of D.C., so all could see like you did that bitch yesterday.

Diego upped his tool, putting it to Fate's forehead. Fate rested his head over the opening of the gun, making sure once Diego pulled the trigger, it would be no room for him to miss. Fate closed his eyes and mumbled a few words, then opened them and stared at Diego in his eyes. "Pull it, nigga, I'm ready."

Tears filled up Diego's eyes.

"Squeeze the trigger, nigga!" Fate barked. Diego's finger applied some pressure on the trigger. "If you're having second thoughts, then it's because in your heart you know that I'm as thorough as they come, and loyal as they be." Fate spoke, still holding eye contact with Diego. Tears fell down Diego's face. He removed the gun from Fate's head. Fate opened his arms wide, and Diego walked into them, then Fate engulfed him in a bear hug. Fate held on to Diego as though he was hugging his own son. "We gonna get through this. We gonna find that money and product. Right now we are two million in the red with the plug. So, when the plug gets here, we got to work a deal with them so we can repay the money we owe and still come out on top."

Fate checked his Rolex while still embracing Diego. A knock came to the door, breaking the men's embrace. "Yeah!" Fate yelled out.

"Weedy and his people are here," Chill said through the door.

"I'm on my way down." Fate adjusted his Rolex on his wrist, and checked the Springfield 45 that was on his hip, and secured it back in its place. Diego was still trying to work shit out in his head. He came to the conclusion that if he found out that Fate robbed his uncle's stash houses, he wouldn't hesitate to shut down his main frame with a bullet to his head.

Fate and Diego descended the stairs and entered the small conference room in Cain's house. Walking in the office brought back memories of his boss. The room was used to seal many deals and, at other times, was converted into a war strategy room. Fate missed Cain dearly, but he had to keep his game face on; he couldn't let the death of Cain cloud his judgement, because he could easily be next.

Once fully walking into the room, Fate was disturbed to see a foreign face sitting behind his boss's desk. Creases invaded Fate's forehead. Fate's eyes met Weedy's. Weedy stood next to the stranger, and behind Weedy stood his bodyguard—Flex—and some shooters that Fate assumed had Canadian mob ties.

"Aye, slim, you need to raise the fuck up from behind my uncle's desk!" Diego advanced, but stopped when the shooters upped their Colts 1911's. Fate grabbed Diego by the arm.

"Hold fast, D, let's see what the lick read!" Fate stated, pulling the hot-headed youngster back. Weedy raised his hand, and the shooters lowered their weapons.

"How's it going, Weedy?" Fate asked humbly, trying to relieve the tension in the room.

"You tell me, Fate, my friend was shot and murdered under your watch. My business partner's funeral line was shot up, and his body was set ablaze for all the world to see, and to be played over and over again on social media. So you tell me how the fuck is going on!" Weedy yelled the last sentence so loud that his body shook.

"Weedy, Cain was like a brother to me—"

"Bullshit, Fate, where them fuckers that murdered Cain? Huh? Where are they if Cain is so much like a brother to you?"

"We working on it!" Fate yelled; his underarms started to sweat.

"Working on it is not good enough. Them bitches are supposed to been dead before it was even time to bury Cain." Weedy started cracking his knuckles. The statement took Fate by surprise. Weedy must have been keeping tabs from afar on Cain.

"We working on it, Weedy," Fate retorted. Weedy just shook his head with a disappointed look on his face.

"Let's get down to business before I do something to make my people back home disappointed." Weedy lit a Cuban cigar. Weedy was a Canadian connect that Cain had met in Vegas. Both of them had bonded through their business dealings.

"As you know, Cain sold the Canadian mob this city. He—"

"That's some fuck shit—My uncle would never sell this city," Diego said, cutting Weedy off.

"It's true!" Fate confirmed, crushing Diego's dream of running the family business.

"It's true. We gave your uncle five million—three in an offshore account, and two mill in cash. This man here is Macleko. He was going to come and regulate the business, but with the way that you all got the Feds crawling around here investigating the joy ride you gave that woman when you dragged her body through the streets, and the retaliation of them setting Cain's body on fire in the middle of the streets, it's too hot for my people to even operate in this city." Weedy's voice was laced with sadness. "However, we can still work something out."

"And what's that?" Jelli stated, opening her mouth for the first time since the meeting started. Weedy looked at how thick Jelli's legs were. Weedy liked how she sat with her legs crossed one over the other. He could see why Cain had chosen her to be his Queen.

"We will let you work off the five million bill over the course of time. When up re-up, yo' pay some on the five mill. But you have to pay the remaining bill of the two million for the last shipment." Once Weedy finished making his point, he took a pull of the Cuban.

Fate was running the numbers in his head. The task could be handled, but the beef with the Red Bottom Squad got to be extinguished. Because you can't make that type of money and go to war at the same time.

"I got something better," Jelli countered with her negotiation. "We keep the five mill. And you can keep the city under your thumb. I will run things from out here with the help of Fate and Diego. I got the two million on deck right now. You keep supplying us and, once I avenge my husband's death, I will remove myself—And Diego will push the Canadian mob product long as you keep him as the face of this city."

Fate was furious. He now knew where Cain's money went.

"It seems like you know a lot about the business," Weedy stated.

"My husband trusted me and taught me well—And besides, I got some shit to make a nigga pillow-talk," Jelli said, uncrossing and recrossing her legs. Weedy smiled; he liked this woman. Weedy could tell Fate didn't like what was transpiring.

"So you said that you have the two mill on hand?" Weedy asked.

Jelli got up and exited the room. A few moments later, she came back rolling two Louis V luggage. Weedy opened the luggage. The Louis V's were packed tight with bluish-green colored 100's. Weedy clapped his hands, praising Jelli's gesture.

"Business is back in motion," Weedy said.

"We would like to negotiate prices with you," Fate butted in

"I don't negotiate prices with the help of a muthafucka who let a group of bitches take down a good friend of mine. Now what I would do is, keep the prices the same as they were when Cain was alive. And if business remains straight, and you all solve y'all problem with the Red Bottom Squad, I would work something with Diego. But to ensure that Jelli doesn't meet the same fate that Cain did, I'm placing insurance on her. Whatever happens to her—best to believe—better happen to you or—" Weedy paused. "That beautiful daughter of yours that attends Bowie State—I think her name is Morea." Fate's eyes flashed with murder, with the mentioning of his daughter. Weedy continued: "Or your mother that resides in Atlanta will experience a horrible death."

Fate understood the type of pressure that he was under. He couldn't reveal his cards. "Whatever happens to her happens to me." Fate took oath. There wasn't anything he could do.

Weedy nodded. "Okay. Since we all got an understanding, Jelli, I expect for you to check in with me weekly. And know once again, I'm deeply sorry for your loss." Weedy left the conference room, two million dollars richer, and with his goons.

Jelli pulled out a Garcia Vega that was already pre-rolled. She sparked it and enjoyed the first few pulls without uttering a word. Diego and Fate watched her closely. "Fate, set up a meeting with all our distributors—I have to talk to the streets. It's time for a real bitch to be heard," Jelli said, blowing out a cloud of smoke.

Chapter 4

Tata shut her phone off. The calls had been coming in non-stop since the news reached the public about how Zoey's body was snatched out the funeral line hearse and ripped from her casket, and dragged from the back of a stolen truck like a rag doll. When the authorities finally relocated Zoey's corpse, her clothes were torn from her body, her head was ground down to almost nothing. People in the city had captured the incident on their phones. Some fucked up individuals had posted it on social media. It was always a new clipping coming in showing Zoey being dragged from different angles through different parts of the city.

The police found Zoey's body nine blocks away behind an abandoned house on Franklin Street, NE. Tata knew that the transgression came from Cain's people. The guns that launched the attack let it be known by the *Rest in Peace* Cain shirts they wore. There was no doubt in Tata's mind that the move was done on purpose.

The mayor was breathing fire down the chief of police's neck to locate those that were involved in both funeral attacks. Retaliating on Cain's funeral was a boss move, but it was reckless. Whip had convinced her to let him place some death capital bloods on Cain's funeral line, in case Jelli or Cain's people wanted to be stupid and do something foolish. And Whip's intuition was right because Cain's people came with the fuckery.

The chief of police had promised the mayor and the public that she would get down to the bottom of the madness.

The police had been questioning Zoey's grandmother, but she came up in the 50's and 60's where the police was just another form of the Ku Klux Klan. So she didn't trust them. However, she made Tata promise her that she will settle the score with the people who killed her baby.

"I know that we got a lot going on, but you got to get your head in the game," stated Whip, breaking Tata's trance.

"I'm focused, Whip!" Tata said, studying a couple descending from a minivan with six children.

"I know that shit with Zoey got you off balance, but this situation would land you in prison with a life sentence if we don't play our cards right. Before we get the call, are you sure that you can't think of anyone that could be behind this shit?" Whip asked, scanning the Silver Spring Mall parking garage.

"I been twisting my brain trying to come up with who and how someone got an audio recording of me and my squad killing Rico. The only person there was Phatmama, me, Jelli, Zoey and Rico. Rico and Zoey are dead. Phatmama is loyal to the soul, so that leaves Jelli. Although, to be honest, Whip, I don't think it's Jelli behind this shit."

Whip wiped his hand over his beehive waves. He was getting frustrated because he was feeling Tata, and didn't want anything to happen to her. He almost flipped his wig when he came out of the bathroom to find her passed out on the living room floor with a burner phone in her hand. He picked Tata up and placed her on the couch. He got a damp towel and placed it on her forehead to make her come back from her fainting fit. He had learned that someone sent Tata a phone with a voicemail on it telling her they wanted five hundred thousand, or they were going to the police with the recording. That's the reason why they were sitting inside Silver Spring parking garage right now.

He wanted badly to know who was behind this, so he could smash them and get back to getting money. Whip texted his team, and made sure they were in place and on point. He and Tata were waiting for the burner phone to ring—the very phone that the ransomer had taped on the windshield of Tata's truck the night Zoey was killed. The goal was to track the money, and that will reveal who's behind the extortion. Whip reached over and touched Tata's thigh, caressing it. Tata welcomed Whip's touch. Having Whip with her made her feel somewhat secured.

The phone on Tata's lap rang, interrupting the sensation that she was experiencing under Whip's touch. Her hand trembled, as she answered the phone. "Yeah!"

"Get out the truck with the money and walk into the mall. Walk around until I call you. If I see shit ain't right, I'm delivering the recording to the police personally." The ransomer ended the call.

Whip heard the whole convo. Tata had the phone on speaker. Whip knew the ransomer was somewhere in the parking lot watching them, because he instructed Tata to get out the truck with the money. His fingers went to work, sending a text to his shooters. "Turn your phone back on and activate your Bluetooth. I'm calling you now."

Tata followed instructions and answered Whip's call. She placed the Bluetooth in her ear and dropped her hair over it, concealing it. She grabbed the backpack off the back seat. Tata made her way into the mall from the top level of the parking garage. The Silver Spring Mall was packed with shoppers. Tata harnessed the back pack in her back, and kept her eyes alert.

"What's going on, Tata? Talk to me." Whip's voice came through the Bluetooth in her ear. Tata was nervous as fuck. She didn't know if anyone was watching her from a distance, so she was hesitant to move her lips and answer Whip.

"I don't see anything but shoppers—I really don't know what I'm looking for," Tata confessed.

"You got your shades with you?"

"Yeah, why?"

"Put them on so if anyone is watching they can't see you scanning the mall for them," Whip instructed. Tata un-hooked her Chanel shades that were clipped to her shirt by the arm of the shades, and slid them on her face. Her eyes were everywhere behind the lens of the shade, trying to see if anyone looked familiar to her, but no one did.

"Whip, I think someone is watching me—I can feel it," Tata said, barely moving her lips.

"Just keep it cool, baby, we can pull this off," Whip stated, reassuring Tata he was with her every step of the way.

The burner phone rang in her hand. "The phone is ring-ing, Whip. I'm about to answer it. "Hello!"

"Keep going until you get to the movie theater." The caller hung up.

"He wants me at the movie theater," Tata conveyed to Whip through her Bluetooth.

Tata made her way to the movie theater. She stopped in front of the movie poster that advertised the movies. She read the previews, trying to calm her nerves. Her heart was racing.

She thought every male that passed her in the mall could be the ransomer. She still couldn't understand how someone got their hands on that recording of her killing Rico.

"Damn, sexy, what's your name?" a tall light-skinned dude asked, with a red Washington Nationals hat pulled low over his eyes.

"Humm, I'm waiting for somebody," Tata said nervously. She studied the mall as if she was waiting for someone.

"I know you are, but Sticks is my name, and Whip is my fam. Whip just wanted you to know that you are not by yourself." Sticks stuck out his hand to Tata who immediately accepted it once she heard Whip's name. She felt better, knowing someone was in the mall with someone that was on her side. Sticks walked away and started window shopping.

"Thank you, Whip," Tata said, still facing the movie posters. "Why didn't you tell me before I left?"

"It's not that important but right now stay focused," Whip stated. The phone rang again in Tata's hand.

"Hello."

"Get in the elevator and get out at the food court on the bottom floor." The caller hung up.

"He wants me to go to the food court, Whip. If I take the elevator, we gonna lose connection," Tata informed Whip.

"Did he say anything about Sticks approaching you?" Whip wanted to know.

"No!"

"Good he don't have eyes on you. Don't take the elevator, take the escalator but hurry up."

Tata started speed-walking towards the escalators. The money on her back started to become heavy. She adjusted the straps on her shoulder. The moving stairs got Tata to the food court quickly, but not as fast as the elevator would have. The burner phone rang again in her hand, and for the third time today Tata answered it. "I'm in the food court, now what?" Tata spoke into the phone loud enough so Whip could hear the one-sided conversation.

"I know you're in the food court, bitch. And I see that your ass can't follow instructions. I told you to take the elevator, not the escalator."

"I get claustrophobia. The elevator would have freaked me out." Tata lied without flaws.

"Rico always said you was a sneaky bitch. Get the fuck in at Pizza Hut and order two large pizzas—one with everything on it, and the other one with just pineapples." The phone went dead. Tata walked over to the Pizza Hut line. Her mind was racing. The person on the phone knew her and Rico personally.

Whip spoke through the Bluetooth: "Aye, Tata, I just got a text from Phatmama. She's outside the mall. She said your sister just parked in a green rental. She just parked on the food court side of the mall."

Tata's mind and heart were operating on overdrive. What were the chances that her treacherous ass sister would be sitting outside the mall where she was paying a ransom for an audio recording of killing Rico—the father of her unborn child. Shit wasn't sitting right with Tata. The person on the phone had her order two pizzas, one of which had just pineapples on it. That was the only way her sister Tina would eat her pizza.

"Tell Phatmama to stay with the bitch—She got something to do with shit," Tata stated in her Bluetooth, as she stepped to the counter and ordered the pizzas.

Ten minutes later, Tata sat at a table with two large pizzas and five hundred thousand inside a book bag at her feet. Her phone rang again. "Yeah," Tata said.

"Get up and leave the food and the money. Go to the ladies room and send me ten pussy and titties pic, and them bitches better be good ones too. I want to see them pussy lips busted wide open. I want to be able to jack my dick to your pic while I spend your money."

"I'm not about to—"

"Bitch, you gonna do it, or I'ma give the recordings to the police."

"Tata looked around the food court. She couldn't see who the caller was. It seemed like every person in the food court had a phone glued to their ear. Tata hesitated. She disconnected the call and made her way to the bathroom that was located by the escalators. She didn't know why the fool ass nigga wanted to humiliate her by making her send him pics of her pussy. But she had to do what needed to be done to keep that audio out the hands of the police.

Tata was happy that the bathroom was empty. She found the end stall, went inside, and locked it. She placed her Glock on the back of the toilet. She kicked her shoes off and removed her left leg from the white jeans she wore. Her white vickies came next. Tata propped her bare foot on the seat of the toilet. She grabbed the phone and started taking pics of her love box. She pulled her folds back on her pussy with two fingers, showing all her glory, and snapped a few shots. She then upped her shirt and released her B-cups from her bra, and took some pics of her breasts. Tata felt sick, but she had to G up. Pulling her shirt back down after securing her breasts in her bra, Tata slid her leg back into her pants, grabbed the Glock, and stuck it in the small of her back. The burner phone started to ring. "Yeah!" Tata said, wiping a tear from her face.

"Thank you!" the caller said happily, disconnecting the call.

Tata rushed out the bathroom and headed towards where she left the money. The money was gone. "Whip!" Tata spoke into the Bluetooth. She didn't even realize Whip had disconnected the call.

***

Once Tata entered the ladies room, an old man sitting tables away from where she was sitting waited a few minutes. He checked his phone, smiled to himself, sent a quick text, then got to his feet and went to retrieve the pizzas and book bag that Tata left behind. Sticks started trailing him. The older man looked over his shoulder towards the ladies room for any sign of Tata.

Sticks could tell that the man was wearing a disguise. The gray beard looked funny on his face, and his body structure was saying he had some youth in him. The guy walked out the mall, and a woman driving a green car honked her horn. The man casually walked over to the waiting green car, opened the back door, and dropped the bag on the back seat, and shut the back door. He then proceeded to open the front passenger door, but a hit with a right hook from Sticks knocked him out cold.

Tina panicked and pulled away from the curb, flooring the rental. The car burned rubber, pulling out. A black van pulled up, and Whip jumped out and helped Sticks throw the old guy in the van.

Phatmama got behind Tina in a stolen GMC. Boot was hanging out the passenger window with a Backwoods cigar hanging out his mouth, and a Glock .40 in his hand. *Boom-Boom-Boom!* The Glock popped off; people on the street ducked for cover. Tina stomped down harder on the accelerator. She couldn't maneuver the vehicle because she was eight-and-a-half months pregnant. A bullet slammed into the rental dashboard, scaring the shit outta Tina. She made a sharp right on the next block, trying her damndest to shake whoever was chasing and shooting at her.

The GMC bent the corner behind her. For the first time, she realized that it was Phatmama in the GMC. Boot let off two more shots Tina's way: *Boom-Boom!* Her front windshield shattered, but it didn't drop. This hindered Tina from seeing. A tightness formulated in her stomach. *Boom!* Another shot rang out, and a second bullet slammed into the dashboard again, causing Tina to crash.

Boot climbed back into the truck, switched his clip for a 30-round clip, and tied his red flag around his face. Phatmama pulled her Michelle Obama mask on, and floored the truck; she grabbed the Mack 11 that rested between her legs.

"Here, handle the business." Phatmama said, handing the Mack 11 to Boot.

Boot grabbed the Mack 11 and turned it on the police cruiser that was pursuing them. It was only one officer in the car; so, if he could stop him, they had a good chance of getting away. Boot aimed at the police car tires and front grill

Yak-yak-yak-yak-yak! The gun danced in Boot's hand. The front tires exploded, and the police cruiser lost control, sideswiping a parked car and getting itself hooked on to another parked car, causing the police cruiser to crash. Boot saw that the cruiser wasn't chasing them anymore. He and Phatmama bent a few corners, where they abandoned the truck after wiping it clear.

Tina's head was ringing; she had a hard time focusing. She grabbed the bag of money off the floor. In lifting the money bag from the floor, the strain in doing so forced her water to break. "Oh shit!" Tina said, putting a hand over her stomach, as she felt the warm liquid run from between her legs. Tina could hear police sirens in the distance. She managed to get out the rental with the money. She was light-headed. A minivan pulled up and stopped. An elderly couple had seen a pregnant Tina wobbling and disoriented in the middle of the streets. The couple had seen the crashed car and put two and two together. The couple exited the van to help Tina.

"Baby, are you alright?" the elder woman asked with great concern in her voice.

"Get me away from here," Tina said. She had a head wound, and blood started to trickle out of it.

"Just sit tight, baby—I'm going to call for help." the woman said, grabbing her phone out the van. The older man helped hold Tina from falling on the ground.

"No! Please, no police or ambulance—Just take me home," Tina begged, opening and pulling out two bricks of money and handed it to the woman with a shaky hand

"No, baby, I can't take your money."

"No, take it." Tina insisted.

The old man wasn't like his wife. He knew money was hard to come by, especially the kind that this woman was offering them. "Wonda, take the damn money and help me get her in the van!" the old man ordered. Wonda just shook her head with a disgusted look on her, and helped her husband get Tina into their van.

Chapter 5

Two days later

"Man, I don't know how y'all feel, but I ain't feeling working for a bitch—I worked for the nigga Cain, not his bitch—I'm from a different breed where we fuck bitches and keep them in their place," Spice said to Cain's elite drug distributors. The twenty men that occupied the auto body shop were responsible for distributing drugs for Cain throughout D.C., Maryland, and Virginia. Many people thought Cain just had shit on smash in D.C., but Cain's movement was bigger than D.C. He had a real empire.

"I'm feeling your vibe, my nigga," Fatts said, nodding with his bottom lip poked out. He had shit sewed up for Cain in a small town called Fredericksburg, VA. "I ain't even bring the money that I owed Cain. I believe in paying my debts, but I don't believe in paying a dead man." Fatts pulled a Newport 100 from behind his ear and sparked it.

Sparko spoke bluntly: "Man, you niggas trippin'. Pay the debt and keep the money train coming in; that way, your family gets fed right along with your team. I don't give a fuck if the bitch is dishing out *work*, as long as the product is straight, the numbers right and she can keep her mouth close. Then shit don't matter to me." He had a section in Springfield VA on lock.

"Nigga, you sound crazy as fuck—How the fuck you think these nigga here gonna respect you if they find out a hoe supplying the work?" Spice said, trying to make Sparko see things his way.

"Spice, niggas respect my G all fuckin' day; that's not even in the question, bruh—A real street nigga respects that bank, especially if the money long—They ain't worrying

37

about who supplying the work; they more concern about how they can get put on, and that's real talk," Sparko said, hoping the pearls of wisdom he just gave Spice will sit home with him. Sparko blazed a cigarillo and put some exotic bud in rotation.

The men stood in an old auto body shop that sat off Benning Road NE. They were waiting for their new boss to arrive. She called a meeting, and everyone had their own idea why she had called the meeting. Some were thinking that she was going to tell them that the plug was dry and no more work was going to be distributed through Cain's crime family. Others thought she was going to continue to plug them and keep everyone eating. And some were thinking Jelli was going to ask for help to locate Cain's killer.

"Damn, it's getting hot as dog shit in this shop—I hope this broad show up soon," Flame said with a little irritation in his voice. He was without his shooters. One of the protocols of this meeting was, you came without shooters and you left all guns in your whip. Flame was a blood that operated out of the Oxon Hill MD area. The small group of bloods out there was doing numbers with the heroin that Cain was supplying. Flame was low-key, and his group of bloods had the same motto as him: "Stay low and make money." But don't get the Flame Boyz twisted; they were ruthless as they came. Flame checked his watch; it read 12:15 p.m. The meeting was supposed to start at 12:00 p.m. Jelli was already late.

***

Jelli sat in the back of Cain's Bentayga. She watched the auto shop from behind the dark tints of the Bentayga. She knew that she was about to venture into no man's land. She knew the only way she was going to be able to crush Tata was to get her money right, and the only way she was going to maintain Cain's empire was by being ruthless and relentless. The day after Cain was murdered, she rushed to Cain's stash houses and cleaned them dry. Cain had six million in the safe, and two hundred bricks. A hundred bricks of coke and a hundred of heroin. Cain had been discussing business with her ever since he had shown her the layout of his organization. Jelli caught on to the operation quickly. That's how she was able to know that the family owed Weedy the two million for the last shipment. What she didn't know about the business, she was sure to learn from Fate and Diego. Jelli didn't have to be a rocket scientist to know the two weren't happy about her gaining control over the family business, but once she gave them a million apiece after meeting with Weedy, then their demeanor changed and they were more open to the idea of her handling things.

Jelli lit the Backwoods, and inhaled deeply. She needed to get her mind right before she went into the meeting and established herself. After the weed started to work, she tapped the driver side headrest, where Fate was sitting behind the wheel of the Bentayga. Fate got out, adjusted his suit jacket, and opened the back door, letting his new boss out.

Jelli's money-green Giuseppe Zanotti stilettos touched the pavement. She balanced her 152 pounds on the four-inch stilettos gracefully. She pulled her black Chanel slacks with the matching money-green pinstripes out her crotch area, but that did little justice stopping the protruding coochie print that was jutting up against the fabric of her pants. Buttoning up her matching suit jacket, Jelli passed the Chanel frames over her brown bubbled eyes. She walked across the street with sassiness and confidence. Fate led the way while Diego brought up the rear.

The men were in the back of the auto shop, kicking the shit when Fate and Jelli walked in along with Diego. All twenty pairs of eyes fell on Jelli; many checked her out, some even stared at how her pants cut between her legs. Sparko held his glare firmly on Jelli's face; he wanted Jelli to see the discipline he had.

Jelli stared into the eyes of each individual in the room. Most of them held lust in their eyes, and wouldn't see her as a boss or an equal business partner. She had to make them respect her just as they would've respected Cain if he was standing in their presence. "Good evening, fellas," Jelli spoke. Many of the men nodded in acknowledgement. Jelli hit her Backwoods again, and removed her Chanels from her face. She plucked the Backwoods to the floor, and smashed it out with the toe of her Zanottis.

"I called this meeting to accomplish a few things with y'all," Jelli said, unbuttoning her jacket: the money-green shirt she wore under it was cut low and showed some cleavage. "First, my man, my husband, still lives on. He lives on through this family. He lives on through the continuance of loyalty. He lives on with every money move that this family makes—" Jelli paused, making sure that the men in the shop understood what she was saying, and where she was coming from. "Cain been good to y'all, and that's obvious because you are his elite distribution team and for you to handle large quantities of his product, he had to trust you and in return you had to show that you were loyal." Jelli caught one of the men rolling his eyes at the statement. She made a mental note and continued her speech.

"This is Cain Crime Family, but make no mistake about it—I run this shit!" Jelli spat with venom. "Let's address the elephant in the room. I could smell the testosterone when I walked in the room. Jelli shook her head in a no-no manner.

The way a mother would do when she caught her child doing something wrong. "My nuts are bigger than anyone in this room." Jelli was cut off by a snicker from Spice—the same nigga she saw rolling his eyes like a bitch. Fate stepped up, but Jelli declined his assistance. Diego leaned against the door, watching the show. He wanted to see how Jelli was going to handle the situation. "Do you have a comment you would like to make?" Jelli asked.

Spice held his silence, as he stared at Jelli indifferently. "Naw, I'm good, carry on," Spice said nonchalantly.

"Alright, business will pick back up next week. Fate and Diego will make sure you all get what you need to continue feeding your team. Do anyone have anything they need to address with me. This will be the last chance that you will have to address me directly. All concerns will be brought to Fate or Diego in the future, and they will bring your concerns to me."

No one in the group spoke up. "Okay—before Cain died, some of you owed this family some money. I ask you all to bring what you owe, so please let me get that." Jelli made that statement with a smile on her face while keeping her eyes on Spice.

Sparko walked up and handed Jelli a Vickie Secret bag. It was loaded with money. Fate retrieved the money, taking a mental note who was paying out and who wasn't. Diego played the door and watched.

"Aye, check this out, Boss lady, a nigga ain't got that paper—I wasn't traveling out here with all that paper without a shooter," Spice said. Sparko shook his head at Spice's stupid ass. Jelli could see the lie in Spice's eyes. This nigga was trying to play her. He was trying to disrespect Cain's name, and she wasn't having it. She unholstered the pink Glock she had concealed in the small of her back. *Boom!* A jagged black hole appeared in the middle of Spice's head. A patch of skull, brains and blood busted out the back of his dome; a mist of blood and gunpowder filled the air. Everyone in the room got low. Sparko didn't even flinch; he just stood there, watching the bloody volcano erupting out the back of Spice's head as he bled out on the floor.

"Do anybody else here owe the family some money?" Jelli yelled with her arms out wide, with her smoking Glock still gripped in her hand.

The hustlers in the room shook their heads in slow motion. Sparko's eyes shone with excitement because he respected Jelli's gangsta. *What a way to make a statement!* Sparko thought.

Flame's scary ass made his way over to Fate, and handed him the money he owed Cain. Flame wasn't feeling how Jelli rocked Spice to sleep. At that moment, he felt she placed everyone at risk, and jeopardized herself and Cain's organization by killing Spice in front of twenty niggas. Cain would never have played his hand like that, but it wasn't his place to school or check Jelli on how she conducted her business. He adjusted the red rag in his back pocket, and watched for Jelli's next move. Jelli reached over Spice's dead body and removed the still burning Newport from between his fingers. She took a long drag of the cigarette. She placed the Chanels back over her eyes. "Meeting adjourned," Jelli said, letting smoke seep out through her nostrils.

***

Tina's eyes misted over, looking down at her handsome new-born son, as the infant feasted in her golden-brown nipple. She smiled at his little cheeks working non-stop to get the milk out her breast. Tina stroked his little cheeks, as he fed. Tina's body was sore from the car accident that forced her into labor. But seeing her son healthy and alive took all the pain away from her aching body. The doctors said the accident had stressed her and the baby, which forced her water to break. God was working with her three days ago. The older couple that helped her get away from the car crash took her to her apartment, which wasn't far from the Springfield mall. They refused to leave her alone in her state. She made them wait in the van while she went inside her apartment to grab her social security card and ID. She then stashed the money inside the air vent inside of her apartment.

Tina returned to the older couple, who proceeded to rush her to the hospital. She was rushed into the laboring room. Tina found out, through conversation with a nurse, that Wonda and Milton didn't tell the police they made a pit stop to her apartment. They told the police they found Tina climbing out a car that was involved in an accident. When the police interviewed Tina, she told them that some young boys tried to carjack the rental she was driving. She added that the reason why she didn't wait for the police when she crashed the car was because she was afraid she may have hurt the baby doing the crash.

Her thoughts turned to Tone. She hoped that he was alright. She saw the skinny dude knock him out cold. She'd never seen someone get hit that hard before in her life. Right before she turned off the street, she caught a glimpse of some goons tossing Tone's body in a van. But then again, she didn't really give a fuck about Tone; he was just a pawn in her life. He was just like every other nigga in the streets of D.C. He was a fucking opportunist. She played with Tone's heart because the dick was good, and he told her everything Rico was into and who he was fucking. Tone's stupid ass really thought the baby was his.

"My pretty boy!" Tina said softly, rubbing her thumb across her son's cheek.

"Hey, mama!" Ski said, walking in the room. "Oh my god! He's so cute." This was Ski's first time seeing her little brother. "He's a hungry little joker, ain't he? Look at him work them little lips on that nipple," Ski said, laughing. Tina didn't say anything. She continued to look down at her feeding newborn. Tina had some things she needed to get off her chest with her daughter—Ski. After Tina was admitted to Howard University hospital on Georgia Ave., she was asked if she wanted her next of kin contacted. She didn't want to be alone, so she had a choice but to call Tata or her sixteen-year-old daughter. Calling Tata was even an option, so she chose to call Ski's scandalous ass.

"Hold still, mama, so I can get my first picture of my baby brother," Ski said, snapping away with her phone.

Tina looked at her crazy ass daughter. Ski took her and the baby's pic. Ski immediately posted the pic on her social media platforms. "Ma, you figured out what you going to name my little brother yet?" Ski asked, putting her phone away. Tina licked her dry lips.

"Rico Sammad Llvans!" Tina replied, making eye contact with her daughter. A burn of hate was roasting in the center of her chest. Ski was her flesh and blood. She knew the girl was out there in them streets chasing money and material things; she understood this because she too had lived that life. But there was only one way that her and Ski could be one again: she had to confront the situation head on to extinguish the hate that was unforgivingly burning within her heart. "Ski, how long you been messing around with Rico?" Tina blurted out. The statement blindsided Ski, but she rebounded quickly.

"Ma, what in the hell you talking about?"

"Don't stand in my face and play me for a dumb bitch because you and I both know I'm way too sharp for that!" Tina retorted. It all came vivid to Ski why her mother had been acting so cold towards her over the past months. "How would you feel if I went behind your back and fuck your nigga—Diego?"

The question sent Ski's hazel eyes a shade darker. "Ma, don't play—that's some disrespectful shit!" Ski protested.

"How the fuck yo' think I feel to find out you been with Rico, the man I love?" Tears started to gather in her eyes. The gash and knot that was on her head, and her tousled hair had Tina looking a mess.

Ski could tell that her mother was hurting about her sleeping with Rico. "Ma, I'm going to be honest. Yeah, me and Rico have been together. It's only been once and it's only been through oral." Ski's voice was laced with sadness. Now she started to cry. "I didn't know that you and Rico was creepin' around with each other until that day Tata and Zoey came to the apartment, and you and Tata had that fight. The day you confessed that you were carrying Rico's baby. That's the God honest truth."

"You telling me that you didn't know that me and Rico was sleeping together? After all those times he came to pick me up in the middle of the night!" Tina yelled, making baby Rico jump in her arms.

"Ma, I never thought you were sleeping with Aunt Tata's man. I just thought you and Rico just got tight and Tata was y'all bond. It never crossed my mind that he was having an affair."

Much as the situation hurt Tina, she knew that she must forgive her daughter. Much as she wanted to continue to hate Ski, she couldn't because—in reality—it was Rico's doing. He knew Ski was her daughter, and he knew she was her mother. Tina didn't want to come to grips that Rico was the one in violation, and not her daughter. The love she had for Rico was real but his for her wasn't. "Come here, Ski," Tina said, wiping wetness from her face. Ski hesitated, but she came over and bent down into her mother's open arm. Tina squeezed Ski tight while still holding baby Rico in her left arm. "I love you, Ski."

"I love you too, Ma."

"This is our family right here—Me, you and baby Rico—No one else," Tina said with her head buried in the crook of Ski's neck. "We must protect this family by all means. Do you understand me, Ski?"

"Yes, Ma, I understand."

"No man—no bitch—comes before us," Tina whispered.

"I agree, Ma," Ski mouthed.

"Now sit up and let me tell you how your auntie tried to have me killed the other day," Tina said, positioning baby Rico so she could hold him.

Chapter 6

"Oh, work that shit, Phat! Long stroke that shit, bae," Boot said. *Bup-bup-bup!* was the sound the fourteen-inch strap-on made when Phatmama slammed the synthetic composite, skin-like strap-on into a badly beaten Tone. "Hula-hoop in that shit, Phatmama!" Boot cheered Phatmama on. He was deeply into that savage shit.

Phatmama had Tone in the back position; she was in a push up position like a nigga would have been if he was putting that pressure on a female. Phatmama pulled about eight inches out of Tone's ass, hula-hooped her hips in a circular motion a few times, then she forcefully slammed down into Tone's asshole. Blood and shit coated the massive strap-on.

"*Unn—Unn—Unn!* was the noise Tone made with every punishing thrust Phatmama gave him. He wished that they would kill him already and get it over with. Phatmama was in a different world; she was zoned out. She didn't give a fuck that she was rocking a sports bra and a strap-on, fucking the shit out a real live nigga in front of her squad. Phatmama was breathing hard with every stroke. Sweat dipped off her face on to Tone's swollen lips and closed eyes. Phatmama had on one of them strap-ons that created friction on the clitoris, and she loved degrading a foul ass nigga like Tone. The degradation put her on the verge of cuming. "You gonna tell me—" Phatmama delivered more thrusts in between every few words—"What I want to know!" Phatmama yelled, banging her pelvis into Tone's bottom. *Bop!* The contact sounded off. "Oh, shit! I'm cuming. I'm cuming!" Phatmama screamed. Boot smacked Phatmama's juicy ass and watched the waves of her back side ride out, as she shook in pleasure. Phatmama locked her pelvis into Tone's, and held it there.

The audience that watched the show was speechless. The group was watching Phatmama and Boot in a different light. Billie had the look on her face, like, "What the fuck!" She had known Phatmama since her military days, and she'd never known that girl had a side of her like this. *This bitch is a real live savage*, Billie thought.

Tata didnt give a fuck what Phatmama did to Tone's hoe ass. All she was concerned about was finding Tina and destroying them audio recording and killing Tina. The act had Racks fucked up for some reason. She wasn't showing sympathy for Tone, but the vile act was messing with her morally. She just knew it was plain wrong for a woman to fuck a man in the butt. Whip didn't give a fuck about Tone or what Phatmama did to him. He was tripping on how excited the nigga Boot was getting by watching Phatmama fuck Tone. He and Boot were definitely gonna have a conversation.

Phatmama pulled the strap-on out of Tone's booty-hole; it made a popping sound upon its exit. The stench of Tone's raw bowels stunk up the air of the warehouse. Billie and Tata put their hands over their noses. Phatmama took Tone's discarded shirt, and wiped the strap-on clean like it was a real dick. Boot walked over and kissed her on her lips. "Muah! You did good, Phat!" Boot said.

"Thanks, babe, he'll talk now," Phatmama retorted, taking the strap-on off and wiping her pussy clean with some wet wipes, and stepping back into her jeans that laid on the floor next to Tone. "Now, Tata, ask your questions again!" Phatmama instructed her boss, who stood there with a stone face. Tata's red bottoms click-clacked against the concrete, as she made her way over to Tone, who laid on the floor—

barely alive and bleeding from the face and ass like a mongrel in a dog fight. Tone's breathing was shallow.

Whip lit a Backwood and watched Tata. He was so fascinated with this black Puerto Rican. Her 5'7 frame was perfect for his six-foot height. Her curves and thickness fitted immaculately into her hundred-and-forty-three pounds, but Tata's overly luscious lips were nothing short of a wonder to Whip and Tata had agreed to keep their friendship under wraps, but it was obvious they both had a thing for each other. When Tata came walking into his trap with a brick of heroin, wanting to hire D.C.B.'s as her shooters, he wanted to tell her no, and to kick rocks, but he couldn't resist the beautiful woman.

Tata squatted down next to Tone's battered head. She had a few questions she needed answers to. "How did the Feds get on to Rico about the off-duty Fed getting killed doing the McCormick & Smith robbery?" Tone struggled to swallow; his mouth was bone-dry. He was afraid that if he lied to Tata, Phatmama was going to put the dick back in his butt, and he didn't want to experience that again. His asshole was on fire, and it felt like it had a heart beat in it.

"I—I sent some jewelry to the FBI with Rico's prints on it from the heist." Tone spoke through heavy breathing. He could barely see out his eyes. He had to tilt his head at a certain angle to see.

"Well, I be damn, that makes sense why the Feds was looking for Rico, and not you and Diesel," Tata said, shaking her head. "The whole time you was the rat and I thought it was Diesel who was the weak in." The group in the room just shook their heads; no one liked a rat. "How did you get the audio of me killing Rico and how do my sister come into play in this shit?" Tone wasted no time spilling his guts.

"I got the recording from your sister, she got it from her daughter—Ski," Tone spoke in pain. This puzzled Tata.

"How the fuck Ski ended up with recording?

"The night you killed Rico, he must've butt-dialed Ski by accident before you killed him. "Tone started spitting blood out his mouth. Tata couldn't believe her luck. *Who the fuck goes to commit a murder and the victim accidently butt-dial a person who knows your voice*, Tata thought to herself. "It was Tina's idea to make you pay the ransom for the recordings." Tone's confession made it obvious why Tina was outside of Silver Spring Mall in the rental. Tata made eye contact with Whip. The look was telling Whip he gotta quickly get his shooters on Tina and Ski.

"Where's Tina?" Tata asked.

"I don't know!" Tone mumbled. "Please don't kill me. Tina's having my baby—don't kill your niece's or nephew's dad," Tone pleaded.

"What! You Tina's baby daddy?" Tata said, looking confused.

"Ye—Yeah," Tone said.

"I'm sorry to inform you, Tone, but Rico is the father of the baby," Tata said, laughing.

"We don't need him," Phatmama said, swiping through her phone. "Tina's at Howard University Hospital. She had a baby boy. Ski dumb ass just posted this shit all over social media." Phatmama handed Tata her phone so Tata could confirm her findings. Whip jumped on his phone and sent Sticks a quick text. Tata smiled at the freshly posted pic of baby Rico, and handed the phone back to Phatmama.

"Kill the rat," Tata mouthed, walking out the abandoned warehouse, leaving Boot and Phatmama to do whatever crazy shit they wanted to do with Tone.

Tata hopped behind the wheel of her Infiniti EX37 Infiniti. Whip got in on the passenger side. Tata let out a deep sigh. The thought of Tina and Ski still having access to that recording was shattering her world.

"Breathe easy, ma—My shooters are on it," Whip said, trying to calm Tata's nerves.

"Whip, I'm not trying to hear that shit right now—All I want to hear is Tina and Ski eulogy at their funeral," Tata said in frustration, as she watched Billie tail-light exit the warehouse parking lot. Tata started the SUV, and exited the lot.

Whip wanted to say something, but he knew the enormity of situation. There was no doubt in his mind that Tina or Ski was going to submit that recording to the police. All he could do was, show Tata that he was going to keep her out them cracka's jail if he had to murder every fucking police officer in America.

Jibril Williams

Chapter 7

Tragedy has plagued the District of Columbia, countless murders have been accruing. But things seem to have escalated after known D.C. Kingpin Cain Ross was executed in the back of an ambulance as he was being escorted to the hospital for gunshot wounds that he received at the Bass & Cru nightclub shootout. The ambulance was stopped by a gunman who gained access to Cain through the back of the rig. A gunman shot Mr. Cain Ross, execution-style. Leading behind this event, Zoey Ray Moore's body was snatched from her funeral line and dragged through the streets like a rag doll. This is the same Zoey Ray Moore who was also a victim of the Bass & Cru shooting. Zoey was found dead in the night club parking lot. She sustained a gunshot wound to the back of the head. In 2012 Zoey Ray Moore was the first African American woman that was tagged as a Golden Glove champion coming out of D.C., after she defeated Shanita Wooten in the 5th round of the Lightweight division. Zoey Ray Moore was convicted of manslaughter the following year of her Golden Glove title. She was sentenced to 6 years. Authorities are trying to figure out how Zoey Ray Moore and Cain Ross's deaths are related, considering that both were murdered the same night, occupied the same club, and both of their funerals were interrupted with violence. Cain Ross's funeral line was shot up, and his body was set ablaze while his body laid inside the hearse. Events behind Cain Ross and Zoey Ray Moore's death have sent chills down the spines of the public, and with all this going on, the D.C. serial killer has stuck again. Tone Lance was found burned to death inside an abandoned warehouse. Mr. Lance's genitals were removed from his body, and placed in his mouth. This seems to be the M.O. of our killer who left Ricky "Bless" Watts dead with his genitals hacked off. The killer left Ricky "Bless" Watts' genitals cooked inside a microwave. The Genital Killer left Ricco Ross dead with a hole in his head and his genitals burned to a crisp—

Jelli almost spat out the wine that she was sipping on while reading the Washington Post on her phone. "Damn, I bet it gotta be Phatmama—this fucking bitch is the infamous Genital Killer." Jelli burst out laughing hysterically. "I knew this bitch was crazy," Jelli said, talking to herself. She adjusted the princess crown on her head. Jelli put the glass of wine on the table, and pulled up her burner phone. She texted: *I know who you really are.*

A text came back: *WHO IS THIS?* Phatmama texted back in all caps.

Jelli chuckled, as she took off the princess crown that bared a black diamond as its centerpiece. She sat it on the table, and took a picture of it and sent it to Phatmama.

***

"Oh fuck! Diego, hmmm, that's my spot right there, papi, hmmm, hold right there," Ski said, sitting on the top of Diego's meat stick.

Diego arched his pelvis and ground his love stick into Ski's love box. Her walls contracted around Diego. The experience was mind-blowing. Ski's young pussy had a way of relieving his mind from the bullshit. He bit down on his bottom lip. Ski laid flat down on top of Diego, stretching her body out. With Diego still buried deep within her, she stretched her arms past his head and sucked on his chin, while she pumped her pelvis up and down on Diego's dick.

Mmmm, mmmmm, mmmmm, was the noise she made as she sped up. Diego could tell she was about to cum, because her walls grew tighter around his wood. He bit down harder on his lip, still holding his body in an arched position and allowing Ski's pelvis to hammer away on him.

"Baby—I'm—cuming. I'm cuming, Diego I'm cum—ing. Oooh!" Ski struggled to get control of herself; the orgasm was catastrophic, but Ski was young and hot. She came off of Diego's wood, making a slurping sound, signifying she was gushing wet. She got into the sixty-nine position. She had to have the pleasure of seeing a man eating her out for her to enjoy it, but she was an aggressive dick sucker. The knowledge of her pussy being sniffed and a nose rolling around in it was all she needed to partake in the position.

Ski lowered her head down on Diego; she slowly licked the length of his dick, tasting and smelling her nectar. She spat on the head. Ski gave the dick a few strokes and spread the saliva over it, then she went straight to muthafuckin work.

Diego closed his eyes, as he felt Ski's warm mouth engulf his manhood. He wrapped his arms around her waist, and inserted his nose in between Ski's crease and made small circular motions around her opening with his nose. Ski started sucking Diego's dick from all different angles. For the life of him, he didn't know she could suck a dick so good; his toes curled and cracked, and this made Ski giggle with the dick still in her mouth. The feeling Diego was receiving was intense. He squeezed a little tighter and pushed a thumb in her ass, and kept sniffing and dipping his nose in the pussy. He was hypnotized by Ski's scent. He worked his thumb in and out of Ski's brown hole. He hadn't invaded Ski's brown hole yet, but this was his way of getting her used to him penetrating her. He had tried to ease his mushroom shaped head into her backdoor in the past, but Ski cried that it was too big and painful, so he started inserting his thumb into her every chance he got, and right now Ski seems to be loving it. She was acting a fool on the dick.

Ski forced Diego's dick into the back of her throat; the gagging sounds she was making egged Diego on the hump up into Ski's mouth. He felt a tingly sensation in his toes, and knew he was about to cum. Ski was sucking the dick to its tip, then slamming back down on it, making the head of Diego's manhood touch the back of her throat. Ski's mouth felt like a vacuum siphoning all the cum out of him.

"Agghhhh!" Diego sounded off, shooting chunks of sperm off into Ski's mouth in three bursts.

Ski continued to suck and stroke Diego's now semi-hard dick; she raised off it as the last remnants of nut rushed to his tip. Ski took her tongue and swirled it around the head of Diego, and got what was left of his man juices.

Diego's head fell back on the pillow; he was trying to catch his breath, Ski crawled her naked caramel colored body on top of his. She threw her thigh over him. Ski started sucking her pussy juices from around Diego's mouth and nose. Diego could feel the head from her coochie on his stomach. That stirred something in him and made his manhood twitch. Ski laid her head in the crook of Diego's neck, and inhaled his scent. His cologne was intoxicating. She played in the sweat puddles that coated his chest. She ran her finger tips through them, enjoying the slickness of his shine. "I love you, Diego."

"I love you too, bae," Diego said, kissing the crown of Ski's head.

"After seeing and holding my baby brother made me want a baby, what you think about us having a little one?" Ski asked with her head still buried in the crook of Diego's neck.

Diego paused for a minute. "What! You must have been watching too much Teen Mom OG," Diego said with a chuckle.

Ski raised her head from its resting place. "No, I haven't been watching no dirty white trailer park trash bitches on MTV, who thinks having a baby as a teen is cool enough to broadcast it on TV to the world," Ski said with an attitude.

Diego chuckled again, palming one of her ass cheeks. "Hold up, I didn't mean it like that. You don't have to go in ya bag on me. I'm just saying, love, we both young. We got a lot of growing to do, and a child is going to slow us both down. A lot of shit is getting ready to happen for me, and all that good shit going to happen is going to affect you as well. We don't want a child slowing up our mojo."

"But after talking to my Ma and her telling me how Tata sent somebody to kill her and she could have lost the baby, I just want to leave something behind if I ever was to die or some crazy shit happens to me."

Something about the way Ski was talking about dying or some crazy shit happening to her made him think of his uncle Cain. He sat up in the bed and placed his feet on the floor; he placed his face in the palms of his hands. His thoughts drifted to how Cain didn't leave a seed behind to carry on his name; he didn't have a son or daughter to carry his legacy on. The only person that was left of the Cain Ross bloodline was him and his mom. The thought enraged him, thinking how Jelli was running his uncle's empire. This got him thinking. *Was this her plan the whole time? Could this bitch conjure up a plan like this*? After all, she and the bitch Phatmama were once friends. Diego shook the thoughts out of his mind. Jelli was on his team; she told the plug that she was turning the city and Cain Empire over to him once Tata was dead. On top of that, she gave him a mill in cash.

"What's wrong, D?" Ski said, scooting behind Diego, and wrapping her legs and arms around Diego's naked body, resting her head on the center of his back. She could hear her man breathing deeply.

"I'm thinking about my uncle. Shit you was saying about leaving something behind sparked some shit in me and my mind doing cartwheels. But I'm feeling where you are coming from though, Ski, and having a baby with you is something that I'm down to do." Diego turned around, facing Ski.

"Oh my God! Diego, are you serious?" Ski became excited, her bare chest jiggled.

"Yeah, baby, I'm serious, because I don't want to leave this earth and leave nothing behind to carry my name on."

"We can get started today, Diego," Ski said seductively. "I got like three hours before I go pick my mother up from the hospital."

"Shit!—That's enough time to make two babies," Diego replied, pushing Ski back on the bed and diving tongue first into her pussy.

Chapter 8

Two hours later

Diego laid in his bed, tired as fuck. Ski drained his ass good. She was dead serious about having that baby, she wouldn't let Diego cum nowhere but inside of her. Diego lit the Backwood that Ski rolled for him before she got into the shower. He took a pull of the Rhino bud, holding it in; the bud immediately set his young lungs on fire. He sat up in bed and let the smoke out through his mouth and nose. Instantaneously, Diego went into a coughing fit. Tears gathered in his eyes, then slid down his cheeks. He wiped the wetness away with his fingertips. "Damn, this shit the truth," Diego said to himself, as he took another pull of the wood. He got up and stepped into his boxer briefs. He checked the G Shock that was on the nightstand next to Ski's phone. Diego picked up Ski's phone and went to the bathroom door. "Aye, Ski, what time you going to pick up your mom?"

"What?" Ski yelled back, sticking her head out the shower, wiping suds out her face.

"What time you going to pick up your mom?"

"At three, why?"

"I was just making sure, but make sure you come straight back to my crib when you pick your mom up. We never know what type of dumb shit Tata and 'em on."

"Okay, daddy." Ski stuck her head back into the shower and started singing.

Diego went through her contacts; he scrolled down until he found the names *Auntie Tata* and *Phatmama*. He then logged the numbers in his phone and placed Ski's phone back on the nightstand. Diego was on a mission to bring that heat to the Red Bottom Squad. "This one right here is for you, Unc."

***

"Ma, I know that you don't want to stay at Diego's crib with us, but it's going to be safe there," Ski said, escorting her mom out of Howard University Hospital.

Ski pushed her mother in a wheelchair; it was hospital policy that all patients be pushed out in a wheelchair upon discharge. Tina felt she was well capable of walking out on her own, but the nurse that was walking with them was there to make sure Tina followed hospital policy to a T. The automatic doors opened on the hospital, as Tina and Ski approached them. The fresh air and the sun rays felt good on Tina's skin; she took in a deep breath.

She felt good being alive and a mother of a second child. She would have enjoyed it better if Rico was there wheeling her out the hospital with their new-born son. Before she left the States, she was going to take baby Rico to his daddy's grave site. So Rico Sr. could meet Rico Jr. The three days Tina had spent in the hospital had placed her in the position to think and replay the events that took place in her life over the past years. She even came to the realization that she was wrong for sleeping with her sister's man, and having a baby by him, but she owed it to her son at least that much, because she had every intention to tell her son the truth about her and his dad. Tina was in deep thought when Ski pulled up in her cocaine-white Infiniti QX60 truck. Seeing the truck made her think about Rico and the day he gave her the truck. Tina had let Ski get the keys to the truck a few days ago, so she could have something to come pick her up in.

The nurse helped Tina out of the wheelchair, and left pushing the wheelchair back into the hospital. Tina thought that she was rude because the nurse didn't even wish her a farewell.

"Ma, I got a baby seat for little Rico," Ski informed her mother.

"Girl, I'm not putting my baby in no car seat yet—I'm going to hold my little handsome man," Tina said, holding her bundle of joy. In her arms baby Rico was sound asleep, wrapped tightly in his mother's arms in a blue blanket. Tina got in the back seat of her truck. "Ski, you better drive my shit like you got some fucking sense too," Tina admonished her daughter.

"Geesh! Ma, I got you," Ski said, getting behind the truck's wheel and pulling out of the hospital parking lot, and headed towards Diego's crib.

"No, go to the apartment first before you get to Diego's crib—I want to get a few things for me and Rico," Tina instructed.

"Come on, Ma, let's go to Diego's spot first, then we can get Diego to come with us later to grab some clothes and the baby stuff you been stocking up for Rico."

"Girl, I'm not going to Diego's apartment without clothes—I don't even have clean panties on, Ski, and Rico don't have shit either," Tina fussed.

Ski understood where her mother was coming from; you just didn't go to people's house that you going to be staying at without clean clothes to wear. Her instinct was telling her to buck her mother's wishes, though. She didn't feel safe at the apartment no more. She hadn't been there since Diego and Zoey had that shoot-out in the apartment. Ever since then, she was crashing at Diego's crib.

"Okay, Ma, but promise me that we'll grab a few things to hold you over for a few days until we can get Diego to ride to the apartment with us," Ski said, looking at her mother through the rear view mirror.

"Okay, fair enough with me," Tina replied, not looking at Ski, but at a sleeping baby Rico Jr. Tina's mind was on the five hundred thousand she had stashed at her apartment in the air vent. She had plans to take the money and start a new life with her, Ski and baby Rico. That was the whole purpose of her giving Ski the nobody-comes-between-us speech.

The drive from Howard University hospital to Tina's apartment was a straight shot up Georgia Ave. to Silver Spring MD. Ski pulled in their apartment complex 15 minutes later. Ski was so much in a haste to get in the apartment and get what her mother needed, she didn't pay attention to her surroundings; if she had, she would have noticed the silver Buick Century parked four cars away, which was occupied by two goons. She hurried around and helped her mother out the back seat of the truck. Even though Tina had her baby, she still walked like she was nine months pregnant. The two ladies walked into the apartment after Ski unlocked the door. The apartment felt stuffy like the air was off or something. "Ma, look what's that?" Ski asked, looking down at the dark brown spots that matted the tan carpet.

"That ain't nothing Ski, it's only blood. I told you after the accident I came home to get my social security card and my driver's license." Tina pushed her daughter farther into the apartment, leaving the apartment door ajar so the stuffiness could air out.

"Ma, you have a seat and attend to baby Rico, and I'll get everything you need."

"Before you do anything, go in the hallway, and look in the air vent and bring me that bag—I got a stash in there, and bring me my gun on the nightstand," Tina instructed.

Ski moved with swiftness. She removed the grill from the air vent, and grabbed the black book bag. The bag was packed and obstinate. She put one of the straps on her shoulder and went to grab her mother's .32 revolver that she kept on her nightstand. Curiosity got the best of Ski as she threw the book bag on her mother's bed and unzipped it. Bluish-green money stared back at her. "Damn, this bitch holding out on me," Ski said to herself with a crease in her forehead. She took three stacks of money and thumbed through the stacks; every single bill in the stack was a 100 dollar bill. Ski laced her waist line with the three stacks, and pulled her Moschino shirt down over her waist, concealing the money. Ski took her phone out and tried to call Diego, but his phone went to voicemail. Her hands had become sweaty, as she texted Diego, letting him know she and Tina had stopped by their apartment to get some things for the baby.

Ski grabbed the bag off the bed and delivered it to her mother who was sitting in the kitchen breast feeding baby Rico. "Here, Ma," Ski said, dropping the bag at her feet and placing the gun on the table next to her. "What do you need now?" Ski asked.

"Go in the hall closet and get the baby blankets, the bibs, them baby socks, and mittens for Rico's hands," Tina ordered. She got up and started removing empty baby bottles out the kitchen cabinet over top of the stove, while baby Rico stayed attached to her left nipple. Tina removed brand new bottle scrubbers from the cabinet also.

"Ma, I got his pampers and everything you asked for," Ski said, as she walked in the kitchen with a trash bag full of the baby items her mother had requested.

"Okay, now go grab me some clothes, a few pairs of sweats and jeans, some t-shirts, socks, panties, make sure that you get some of my cosmetics!" Tina said, placing the new bottle and bottle brushes in the bag that Ski laid on the table.

Ski stuffed as much stuff as she could in a duffle bag she got out of her mother's closet. She was ready to get out the apartment. She wondered why Diego hadn't texted her back yet. She slung the duffle bag over her shoulder, and made her way towards the kitchen where her mom and baby Rico were waiting. "I got everything, Ma," Ski said, as she turned into the kitchen.

Tina was just putting the .32 revolver in the bag with the money. "Okay, I'm ready, let's—" Tina's words were hindered, seeing the two goons standing behind Ski. Tina had made the mistake of leaving the front door open. Ski caught a glimpse of her mother's face. It was like Tina was a deer that got caught in a driver's headlights. Ski felt a presence behind her; she turned around, dropping the duffle bag to the floor. The loud thump from the bag falling and hitting the floor made baby Rico jump.

Pound slapped the fire outta Ski, knocking her to the floor; her vision became blurry from her tears of pain.

"Please don't," Tina pleaded with the man holding the gun to her. "I just had a baby, he needs his mother," Tina said crying.

Sticks stood watching Tina with unforgiveness in his eyes. "I'll tell you what, I came here for two reasons—One, for the money that you took from my boss lady Tata, and them audio recordings that you hung over Tata's head to get that money," Sticks said.

"I don't have no money," Tina said.

"Bitch, do I look stupid? Do I look like I came to play games, huh? Pound, strip that bitch!" Sticks ordered. It was Pounds pleasure to strip Ski; he'd been standing over her, admiring the way her jeans hugged her curves.

"No, no, please, no, she only sixteen!" Tina said through sobs.

Ski tried to fight Pound off by kicking at his arm and hands. A right hook from the 300-pound goon surrendered her. Pound tore her clothes from her body effortlessly. He snatched Ski's bra off, and her D-cup breasts bounced from the force of her bra being ripped off. Pulling her shoes off, he pulled her jeans off with one swift motion. The three stacks of money remained stable around Ski's waist, they were held firm by the band of her boy shorts.

"Oh, shit!—Look at this," Pound said, peeling the money from Ski's waist. "I thought you didn't know what I was talking about?" Pound said, throwing the stacks of money in Tina's face; the money hit Tina in the mouth, and the force from it made her cry harder. Rico Jr. still greedily stuck firm to Tina's breast, as if it was his last meal.

Pound went back and yanked Ski's panties off; instantly he could smell her scent, which aroused him to the point he started to get a hard-on. "Damn, Sticks this little bitch a bad muthafucka," Pound said, bending down and opening up Ski's legs so he could get a better look at her meaty mound. Even out cold, her pussy was loaded and glazed over with her juices.

"Please don't do this," Tina said through tears.

"Blood, back the fuck up!" Sticks said. He didn't like how Pound's big ass was acting like a creep. He came here to kill and retrieve the audio recordings, period.

Pound looked over his shoulder at Sticks. "Come on, Blood, I'm just having some fun," Pound protested.

"Nigga, we got work to do. We don't have time to fuck off. Now, back up and grab this heat."

Pound ran his middle finger through Ski's folds; when he stood up, he smelled his finger and adjusted his dick.

Ski started to gain consciousness. Pound grabbed the .357 from Sticks, and turned it on Tina. Sticks grabbed Ski by her ankles, and pulled her to the middle of the living room. From where Tina was sitting in the kitchen she could see into the living room. Sticks placed Ski on her back with her arms slightly apart from her body. He stood on both of her hands with all his weight; the sole of his Timberland boots bit into the flesh of Ski's hands. Sticks removed the crowbar that was looped in his Gucci belt.

"Bitch, if you scream I will kill you and the baby," Sticks said, raising the crowbar above his head. Ski was just coming through; her eyes were unfocused at first. She tried to move her arms, but they were pinned down by her hands. Finally, her eyes came into focus; she looked up and met the eyes of Sticks. Sticks balled his face up into a ball of anger, and brought the steel crowbar down on Ski's head, cracking her skull. He brought the bar up again and brought it back down on Ski's head with so much force that the claw on the crowbar got lodged in Ski's head, but that didn't hinder Sticks' assault. He worked the bar up and down in Ski's skull until it came free; the crowbar was covered in brain matter, hair and blood. Ski's body shook violently, before her bowels broke, and piss and shit saturated the carpet underneath her.

Sticks stepped off Ski's hands. He made his way over to Tina, who just purged her hospital breakfast on the side of the chair she was sitting in. Sticks brought the crowbar along with him; it dripped with Ski's blood. "Now I'm going to ask you again, where is the money and them audio recordings?" Sticks said, leaning over in Tina's face; he could smell the stench of her vomit on her breath.

"Them monies right here," Tina said in an ineffectual voice, kicking the book bag over to Sticks with her feet.

"See, was it that bad? Now the recordings?" Sticks asked, as Pound was standing behind Tina with the gun trained on her; he was fighting not to faint. He had never seen no shit like Sticks just put down.

"On my phone," Tina mumbled.

Sticks removed Tina's phone and went through it, and found what he was looking for. "Who else got this?" Sticks asked.

"Just me and Ski," Tina admitted truthfully, swallowing the spit in her mouth and snorting up the snot that started to dribble out her nose.

Sticks walked to Ski's discarded jeans that Pound snatched off Ski's body; he frisked through her jeans until he found what he was looking for. He needed to pull a thumb print to gain access to the phone, so Sticks bent down and applied Ski's still warm thumb on the screen of the phone. The phone scanned Ski's thumb and gave Sticks the access to the phone. Immediately, he found what he was looking for. He looked at Pound, and threw up his b's on his right, and announced *Suu-Wuu*. Pound quickly grabbed Tina's head at the top and her chin, and forcefully snapped it to the right; a cracking sound was heard, and Tina was dead before she even realized it.

"What you want to do about shorty, blood?" Pound asked, referring to baby Rico that was still sucking on his mother's breast.

"Leave the lil' nigga," Sticks instructed.

Pound grabbed the stacks of money that he had thrown at Tina, and put them in the bag with the rest of the money.

Ski's phone vibrated in Sticks' hand; a text came in from Diego. Sticks smiled a devilish grin; he opened the text, and his smile was quickly wiped away.

Chapter 9

"Aye, Slim! This is some boss shit, bruh. To think about this shit, you must've really had your thinking cap on, Slim!" Sess said excitedly, as he watched the screen of Diego's phone. "I didn't even know these muthafucka's created an app that can track your phone through Google map."

"A boss gots to move like a boss, I'm going to be running this shit soon," Diego said, pushing the midnight blue Charger through Hanover MD. He checked his mirrors; his gloved hand gripped the wheel tightly.

"This must be how my baby mom found me at the telly with them two hoes a few weeks ago, Slim," Sess said, still watching the screen of Diego's phone.

Diego had downloaded an app on his phone that allowed him to track and locate a person's phone; he'd overheard some chicks talking about the app while standing in line at Ben's Chili Bowl. He volunteered to pay for their meals and gave them $20 apiece, for the young ladies to show him how to download the app and how to use it. All three women informed Diego that he could use the app to track either one of them any day. All three women logged their numbers into Diego's phone, which he quickly deleted once they were out of his presence. Equipped with the spyware technology Diego put it to use. He placed Phatmama and Tata's number in the app, and he got a hit. Phatmama's phone wasn't on, so the app couldn't locate her whereabouts. He got a hit on Tata's number, however, and he was on his way to smash her pretty ass. He was hoping that Phatmama was with her. He could drop both bitches at the same time.

"Aye, fam, you got a call coming in, it's from your bitch—Ski," Sess said, looking at Ski's picture that popped up on Diego's screen.

"Send it to voicemail," Diego said.

Sess hit the voicemail icon, sending the call to voicemail. Moments later, a text came in from Ski, informing Diego that she had left the hospital with her mother and they stopped by their apartment to get her mother and brother some clothes. Sess read the text to Diego.

"Damn, that girl is so hard headed. She's supposed to have left the hospital and come straight back to the crib." Diego banged his gloved fist on the steering wheel.

"Fuck it!" Diego spat.

The Google map showed that Tata was at the restaurant on Hanover MD. The restaurant was called Blue Dolphin. He knew the place; it was one of his mother's favorite spots to eat.

"What's the game plan, Slim?" Sess asked, eyes still glued to the phone screen.

"We drop the bitch where she stands and whoever with her—We can't play with this bitch, Sess, this bitch will ride that trigga," Diego said, firing up a Newport 100 and passing one to Sess, who accepted.

"Man you ain't got to tell me about this bitch. I don't have any intentions on letting this bitch 'X' me out the game. I know she have to be a handful if she had the big homie Cain dropped." Sess started hitting the jack hard, watching the screen.

Diego felt a certain way about the statement Sess made about his uncle getting dropped; he would address that shit later once the mission was over. He chose Sess for the mission because he had an 'A' plus shooting game. He and Sess had put in some work a few times for his uncle; that's how he met the bumpy face dude who stood 5'9, with dark grey eyes and long cornrows that came down past the base of his neck. Sess was twenty years old, two years older than him. Another reason why Diego liked the brown-skinned goon, besides his shooting and murdering game, was because of that mission that Cain had put them on in the past. Sess always let Diego run the show, and that's how Diego liked it. Turning into the Blue Dolphin parking lot, and turning down Tee Grizzley that was coming through the stolen Charger speakers, he grabbed the phone and texted Ski.

***

"Shit! This shrimp and steak plate was the truth." Whip started licking the shrimp juices off his fingers. "I didn't know the Blue Dolphin was doing it like this, I would have brought my baby out here to wine and dine." Whip smiled, showing off his pearly whites.

The Blue Dolphin was an upscale restaurant that all the up and becoming bosses took their loved ones to, in order to have a good time.

Tata smiled back at Whip. "You haven't tasted nothing; you need to taste this stuffed bell pepper. It's stuffed with shrimp, crab, dressing, and three different cheeses." Tata scooped some of her stuffed bell pepper with her fingers, and fed Whip a sample of her dinner.

Whip went overboard, and wrapped his tongue around Tata's fingers, and sucked them. Whip's tongue sent a tingle in between her legs, and she immediately clamped her thighs together, remembering the last time that Whip blessed her with some top piece; Whip's head was the boss.

"Wow! Tata, I'm feeling that, I might have to try that on the next go around that we slide through."

"Are you talking about the bell pepper or me? The way that you had my fingers in your mouth, it seemed you was tasting me too." Tata threw that out there, she didn't want Whip to think he got one on her by sucking on her fingers.

"Well, since you ask, you taste much better than the stuffed bell pepper," Whip replied.

Tata opened and closed her legs, it had been a while since she had some pressure, and after going through all the bullshit with Tina blackmailing her, and Zoey's death, she had been under so much stress. Maybe getting the cobwebs knocked off her pussy will relieve her of some stress. Tata looked at Whip's face. He was handsome but he was different, looks-wise, from any street nigga she ever seen. She never met a dude who wore bifocals like they were Versace frames, but Whip had grown on her. Even though they agreed to just let whatever happen between them happen, she had developed feelings towards Whip. "Say, Whip, let's say that we get outta here and go back to my place and have me for dessert."

"Shit! I thought you would never ask," Whip stated with delight in his voice. "Shit! You owe me."

"I owe you?" Tata said, confused.

"Hell yeah, you owe me, the last time we was together you got yours, and I didn't get mine due to Zoey and Racks came bangin' at your door."

"Well, that's not my fault, you should have been a minute man and you could have gotten yours," Tata said, smiling. "And who gets in the pussy for the first time and try to make love. Where they do that at?" Tata said with a chuckle.

"Whatever!" Whip said, getting a little hot around his neck. He waved the waitress over. "Can we have the check please?" Whip asked.

"Will that be all, sir?"

"Yeah, that would be it." Whip reached into his pocket, and removed a few bills, and gave them to Tata. "When she comes back with the check, pay the bill. I'm going to the bathroom."

"Okay and I'll meet you at the car," Tata replied.

Whip got up and walked to the bathroom; standing at the urinal, he started draining his pipe. His thoughts went to how he was going to be diggin' in Tata's guts in a minute when he got her back to her place. He slowly started stroking his beef stick while still pissing. The phone in his pocket vibrated; he removed the phone from his pocket and saw it was Sticks calling him. He hit the talk icon button. "Suu-Woo, what it do, blood?"

"The nigga Diego is tracking Tata through his phone through an app; he got her boxed in at the Blue Dolphin!" Sticks yelled in the phone.

"Fuck!" Whip said, as he disconnected the phone, pulling his meat back into his pants as he ran out the bathroom. He looked towards the table where he and Tata were having dinner, and she was gone. He peeped Tata leaving out the restaurant. He ran behind her.

Tata walked across the parking lot. The Moët that she had with her dinner, had her buzzing and feeling sexy as well as horny. Her mind was consumed by Whip's King-ding-aling; she became a little flushed from thinking of all the nasty thoughts about Whip. She was so preoccupied with thoughts of getting laid, that she didn't notice the masked figure getting out the midnight blue Charger, with guns raised.

"Tata, get down!" Whip yelled, running out the Blue Dolphin with his chrome 45 in his hand.

Boom! Boom!'

Whip didn't hesitate to let his gun bark. The crackling of Whip's gun made Tata's whole body jerk with panic, but the hollow points from Sess's Ruger made Tata buckle once two bullets struck her. One in the left bicep, and one in between her thighs. One of Whip's slugs smashed into Diego's midsection, dropping him. Diego's trigger finger went happy on his Glock.

Blocka! Blocka! Blocka!

He was shooting aimlessly and out of fear; nevertheless, Whip still had to take cover between some parked cars. He peeked around the car, and saw Tata laid out in the middle of a puddle of blood formulating under her. From where he was, he could see the rise and fall of Tata's stomach.

'Boom! Boom! Boom!

The masked man sent shots Whip's way. Whip got back low and checked his clip; he counted five bullets in his clip. He slammed the clip back home, and took a deep breath. He heard an engine roar to life, and a dark Charger shot past him. Whip knew that it was the goons. When the car shot past, Whip emptied the last five shots into the car. The car kept moving, so Whip knew he didn't hit anything, he ran over to Tata.

Tata looked up at Whip with tears in her eyes. "Help me, Whip!"

"I got you, baby!" Whip said, tucking his gun and scooped Tata up in his arms. It was so much blood on the ground, he just knew that Tata was going to die. He got Tata into the passenger side of her truck, hopped behind the wheel, and murked out. He called Phatmama on the phone. "Yo, mama, Tata been shot!" Whip stated on the phone when Phatmama answered.

"What you mean Tata been shot?" Phatmama yelled.

74

"Some nigga tried to 'X' her, I'll take her to P.G County hospital. She's been shot in the leg and arm."

"No, take her to Billie's house, I'm texting you her address—I'll meet you there," Phatmama said, disconnecting the phone.

Whip glanced at the address Phatmama sent him, and pushed the SUV peddle to the metal.

Jibril Williams

Chapter 10

Sess snatched his mask off his face. "Fuck, fuck, fuck, fuck!" he said, punching the dashboard of the Charger.

He looked over at a bleeding Diego, who sat in the passenger seat—holding his stomach. It felt like his insides were being sliced open with a thousand hot razor blades; Diego faded in and out. Even though the A.C. was on in the car, Sess was still covered in sweat; he could feel it trickle down his back. "Come on, dog, stay with a nigga—G up, nigga, you going to pull through," Sess stated, trying to will Diego to fight for his life.

As he zipped through traffic, he didn't know where he was going. He knew that he couldn't go to the hospital. Every shooting must be reported to the police, 'twelve' will come asking questions, and they would link the Blue Dolphin shooting to him. Spending time in them crackas' jail wasn't on his to-do list. "Where's your phone at, D?" Sess asked for a second. Diego wasn't comprehending what Sess was saying.

Finally, Diego reached in his pocket and removed the phone, and handed it Sess. The phone felt like it weighed five hundred pounds in Diego's hand that trembled heavily. Sess grabbed the phone and wiped Diego's blood from the screen; Sess called Fate. The phone rang four times before Fate answered.

"Nephew, what's good?"

"Naw, Fate, this ain't Diego, this Sess."

"What the fuck you doing with Diego's phone?" Fate said, getting alarmed.

"Man, the little nigga got pop, he bleeding out, I can't take him to the hospital."

"What!" Fate yelled into the phone. "Listen, nigga you bring Diego straight to this location, and don't your ass leave until I get there you hear me?"

"Yeah, I hear you. What's the location?"

"I'm sending it to you through text."

"Alright, bet." Sess hung up the phone. He looked over at Diego, who was fighting to stay alive. "Hold on, bruh, hold the fuck on."

***

Whip pulled up at Billie's house. It was a small little house out in Capitol Heights MD on F street. During the drive over, Billie had called and informed Whip to tie something around Tata's leg above the gunshot wound; that would slow the bleeding, or stop it. Whip rushed over to the passenger side to get Tata out the truck, as Billie rushed out her house to assist him, but Whip lifted Tata in his arms effortlessly. The white Chanel pants that Tata wore was a bloody mess; damn near the whole right pants leg was a dark burgundy color.

"Oh my god!" Billie mumbled; she ran out and got the door for Whip. "Bring her to the basement!" Billie ordered and led the way.

Whip looked down at Tata in his arms; seeing Tata's eyes roll and unroll from the back of her head made him want to murder the world. A part of him felt like he didn't protect her.

"Come on, baby, hold on, just hold on, Mami," Whip said, planting a kiss on Tata's forehead, making it down stairs in the basement; it was like a small medical clinic. It had all types of hospital monitors and equipment and medical supplies. Whip laid Tata on the table, and Billie went to work; she washed her hands thoroughly in the sink in the corner of the basement. She placed on a mask and latex gloves. She already had tools and supplies laid out and ready to go. She then cut Tata's pants and shirt off her with a pair of medical scissors. Tata laid there in a pink lace pantie and bra set. Billie checked Tata's arm wound. "Not bad," she mumbled, as she cleaned Tata's wound with a dark solution, and wrapped it tightly in medical gauzes. She then went and checked Tata's leg wound. "Shit," she muttered.

"What?" Whip asked with concern in his voice.

"The bullet is still in her leg, and the bullet may have broken up into a few pieces."

"Now what?" Whip asked.

"I have to go in and get them."

"We need to take her to a real hospital," Whip said, pushing past Billie.

Billie bumped him. "Whip, I got this. If we take her to the hospital, that's going to open a whole can of jail time."

"But you not a doctor."

"Ya, right, I'm not. Before I went to the military, I was a RN, and once I was in the service I went back to the medical field. So I done learned some doctor trades out there in the battlefield dealing with gunshot victims. Now let me fucking work." Billie pushed Whip back.

Whip stepped back and watched Billie do her thing. She inserted an IV into Tata's arm, a morphine drip.

"Whip, Phatmama going to be here in a minute, please wait for her upstairs."

Whip was skeptical, but he exited the basement.

"If you need a drink or some bud, it's under the sink," Billie said, as Whip walked up the basement steps.

Whip found the kitchen and retrieved a bottle of Cîroc from under the kitchen sink; he twisted the cap off and turned the bottle up, taking in big gulps. The vodka burned as it rushed down his throat, but he welcomed the burn. Whip brought the bottle down, and sat at the small table. He took his gun off his hip and laid it on the table.

Phatmama came rushing in the house with Boot. "Where is she at, Whip?" Phatmama asked.

"She's downstairs in the basement," Whip retorted.

"How bad is it?"

"She took one to the arm and one to her inner thigh. Billie said something about the bullet breaking up in her thigh, and she is going to have to go in and remove the bullet fragments." Whip took another swig of the Cîroc. Phatmama went to the basement to check on Tata.

"You good, blood?" Boot asked, pulling out a pack of Backwoods and twelve grams of some Cali Diesel, and got to twisting up.

"I'm good, blood, just want ole girl to be alright," Whip said, taking another swig from the bottle.

"That's your boo, huh?" Boot said with a smile.

Whip caught the gesture. "Nigga, I know that you ain't talking, nigga, like a nigga don't see you playing Phatmama close."

"Shit! Phatmama complemented my gangsta, blood, we are something that's meant to be," Boot said, blazing the Backwood.

Before Whip could reply, Phatmama came back into the kitchen. "What happened, Whip?" Phatmama asked.

Boot passed the wood to Whip, and started rolling up another one. Whip took a long pull of the Diesel, and let the smoke out through his nose. He looked down at his hands and clothes; they were stained with Tata's blood. The sight alone made him want to murder. "We were at the Blue Dolphin finishing up dinner and I went to the bathroom. Tata told me she would meet me at the car." Whip took another pull of the Diesel and exhaled the smoke. "I got a call from Sticks saying that Diego was outside the restaurant ready to splack Tata. He said something about he was tracking Tata through her phone. I ran out the bathroom and I made it outside. They had already gotten the drop on Tata, I got to bangin'. I dropped one, Tata took two shots and fell."

"We need to find out how Sticks knew about Diego tracking Tata, and how he knew she was at the Blue Dolphin."

"I got blood in route here now," Whip stated.

A knock came at the door; Phatmama went to get it. She came back with Racks, Sticks, and Pound. Phatmama was filling them in on Tata's status, as they walked into the kitchen. Sticks dropped a bag at Whip's feet. Whip knew that was the money bag that Tone took from Tata. That could only mean one thing: Tina was dead.

"Sticks, please tell me how you knew that Diego was tracking Tata's phone." Whip asked.

Sticks pulled Ski's phone out of his pocket and handed it to him. "It's all in the text to Ski," Sticks stated.

Whip read the text message and passed the phone to Phatmama. "Listen, I want everyone to have a new phone and numbers by tomorrow," Phatmama said. "Diego must have gotten Tata's number from Ski. I'm going to kill this bitch."

"No need to—The deed is already done, as well as her mother," Sticks said, as he pulled Tina's phone out of his pocket. "The audio recordings are on their phones." Sticks passed the phone to Phatmama.

She respected Sticks' gangsta. She removed the bag from between Whip's feet, and dug in the book bag, and removed $250,000. She gave Sticks and Pound a hundred and twenty-five K apiece. Sticks tried to refuse it, but Phatmama wouldn't allow him. Sticks and Pound gave Whip 25,000 K apiece.

Two hours later, Billie came into the kitchen with the news that Tata was going to be alright. If her wounds don't become infected, she informed them, Tata was going to need extensive rehabilitation with her left arm because the bullet tore up her bicep pretty badly. But most important was, Tata needed as much rest as possible.

Chapter 11

Sess lifted his head up out of his palms, when Fate walked out the backroom. He was irritated that Fate had him held up in a private practice clinic out in Temple Hill MD. Sess's irritation showed on his face, Fate could sense it. Fate unrolled the sleeve of his Michael Kors shirt and buttoned its cuffs. He eyed the street punk with malice. Sess locked eyes with Fate and didn't break eye contact. Fate sat next to Sess on the edge of his seat, and cracked his knuckles. Fate took a deep breath and exhaled before he spoke. "Sess, what the fuck you and Diego was doing out there?" Fate asked, barely in a whisper; he wasn't trying to lose his cool.

Sess sat on the edge of his chair. "D called me up and said he had a mission that he wanted me to ride out with him on," Sess said, wiping the white gook from the corner of his mouth that was a result of him having cotton mouth. "The little nigga said he had twenty bands for me. So I was, like, fuck it, let's ride. We snatched a stolen whip and went lurking. Diego had some type of crazy ass app on his phone that let him track the broad Tata's location."

"You muthafuckas went on a mission to hit Tata!" Fate was getting more exasperated then he already was.

"Yeah, we went at the broad who had Cain killed, D put twenty racks on her head, and I was trying to cash in on it."

"You should have checked in with me!" Fate retorted.

"And what that mean, old head? I got to check in with you every time I got to body a bitch in this city? When a nigga start doing that?"

"Nigga, anything dealing with this family must be checked with someone of authority."

"Yeah, that's all good," Sess said sternly. "But you forgot, Fate, I'm not part of the family, I'm just a nigga that eats by bangin' his gun, and from what I'm hearing, you ain't the head of the Cain Empire. The broad Jelli, his wife, is."

Fate quickly upped his gun on Sess, and pointed it in Sess's face. Sess showed no fear; he looked Fate in the eye. Fate removed Sess's gun from his hip.

"Let me ask you something, Fate, if I was back there laying on that table, would you have Diego up here with that gun in his face?" Sess asked.

Fate knew where the youngsta was coming from with his question.

"Fate, get that gun out his face," Jelli said, walking out the hallway where Fate and Sess were sitting. They could see Jelli standing in the hallway." From what I heard, he's not the cause of Diego getting shot, but I would like to hear the rest of his story as to what happened," Jelli stated, taking up a seat on the other side of the waiting room clinic, and crossed her legs.

Fate hesitantly took his gun out of Sess's face. Sess stared at Fate with hate, but he continued to tell his story. "Like I said, we was tracking Tata through an app on Diego's phone, the Google map showed that her phone was pinging out of Hanover MD at the Blue Dolphin restaurant. So we crept through masked up, we got there and five minutes later Tata came strutting out. Me and D went to make our move. We had her in our sights, but some cowboy ass nigga came running out the Dolphin bussing. Slugging Diego in the stomach. I was able to put some hot ones in Tata's ass before we got outta there." Sess spoke those last words of his statement with a little happiness in his voice.

The news made Jelli smile. "Do you think she's dead?' Jelli asked, sitting up on the edge of the chair.

Sess put his head down. "Naw, I don't think so," Sess said truthfully.

"Don't worry about it, you'll get another chance," Jelli confirmed.

Sess nodded. "How's he doing?" Sess asked, nodding towards down the hall where he knew Diego was.

"He will be fine, he's young and strong—I think his pride will be more hurt once he finds out he will be shitting in a bag for a while," Jelli said, getting up and walking out the room.

***

"Hush, sssshhh! Don't cry, baby, it's going to be alright," Phatmama said, as she stood in front of Sherman naked.

Tears rolled down Sherman's face while he sat in the chair naked with his hands tied behind his back. The situation with Tata being shot made Phatmama want to kill something. She wanted someone to feel her pain. She had a chance to see Tata before she left Billie's house. Tata gave orders to stand down and not to retaliate until she got back mobile. Phatmama was honoring Tata's orders, but Tata didn't say anything about her activating the Genital Killer. Sherman was a poor soul that Phatmama pulled up on coming out the club, and asked if she could have the pleasure of making his toes curl with some good oral. And just like many niggas that couldn't resist getting their pecker sucked, Sherman jumped on the chance of Phatmama performing fellatio on him. Which led him to be knocked over the head by Boot and strapped to a chair. Boot sat in a chair, watching Phatmama's ass jiggle, stroking the baby arm between his legs. He smoked a Backwood at the same time watching the show.

Phatmama walked around Sherman, she stopped in front of him. She propped a foot up between his legs, and started stroking her love box. "You want some of this, Sherman? Hmm." Phatmama ran circles with her fingers around her clit, she pushed two fingers inside and pulled them out. Boot could hear the wetness from where he was sitting. The taboo shit had him ready to bust all over the place; he had to lay his pipe on the side of his leg and focus on the Backwood he was smoking.

"You want a taste, huh?" Phatmama asked a tied up Sherman, who viciously shook his head by way of saying no.

He couldn't speak because the black ass nigga had stuck a sock in his mouth, because he was crying too loud.

"How about a sniff?" Phatmama said, placing her fingers under Sherman's nose. He turned his head away, which slightly offended Phatmama. She hit him across his jaw with a slap jack. The pain shot up Sherman's jaw line, making his ears ring, the eyes watering, adding to the tears that was already running out Sherman's eyes.

Phatmama walked over to Boot and placed her fingers under Boot's nose; he eagerly inhaled her scent. Her natural scent excited him; Boot engulfed Phatmama's fingers with his mouth and sucked her fingers clean. He closed his eyes and savored the taste. Phatmama dropped between Boot's thighs and took hold of his pulsating Jimmy Dean sausage, and slowly stroked him. Boot and Phatmama locked eyes, and it seemed to be only them in the room. They'd somehow forgotten about the tied up victim in the chair watching them.

Phatmama kissed Boot's dick head sloppily. She swirled her tongue in his peehole, making him twitch in her hands; she loved the feeling of his manhood thumping under her grasp. She worked Boot halfway in her mouth with a slow up and down motion; Boot let out a sigh of pleasure. Phatmama's mouth was so wet and warm like an amazing pussy. Phatmama pulled him out the confinements of her mouth; his dick was heavily coated with her mouth juices. Phatmama puckered her lips and blew on Boot's chocolate pole. Her warm breath created a sensation in his rod that made it swell an inch thicker and added on to his four inches of width. Now Boot really understood the meaning of a blow job; his toes cracked as Phatmama placed him back in her mouth and repeated the process.

Boot took a pull of the Backwood, watching Phatmama intensely. Being with her was like the adrenaline rush a man would get stepping in a cage with a trained tiger for the first time. You don't know if the cat will destroy you or run over and lick you, but its beauty had a way of drawing you near it. That was the effect Phatmama had on Boot. Phatmama popped his chocolate dick out of her mouth, and intercepted the Backwood he was smoking on. She took several tokes from it while slowly jacking Boot. He was mesmerized by Phatmama and geeking for the pleasure and pain she was about to give him. Phatmama let the smoke seep through her nose and mouth. She placed Boot back in her mouth, giving him some hefty licks and sucks, getting Boot back brick hard. She brought Boot out her mouth again, but this time she blew the ashes from the tip of the Backwood. The cherry on the tip of the Backwood glowed brighter. Phatmama licked the inside of Boot's navel before she slightly dragged the cherry of the Backwood across his navel, you could hear the sizzling sound of the heat to skin contact. "Aggh!" Boot let out a moan of pain and ecstasy.

Phatmama squeezed at the base of Boot's manhood, keeping him swollen. She slapped the dick against her cheek and put it back into her mouth. Boot was breathing hard with his back arched in the chair, Sherman watched the satanic scene. He cried in his bounds. All he wanted was to make it home to his wife and kids. Phatmama hit the Backwood again, bringing the cherry to life. She inserted it against the skin of Boot's navel, and that sizzling sound reappeared, causing Boot once again to arch his back and cry out in pain. Boot had a thing for torture and pleasure; the two feelings made him feel alive. The experience was something that was forced on him at an early age. When Boot's mother abandoned him at the age of nine, she dropped him off at his aunt Stacey's house under the pretense that she was going to work and would pick him up when her shift ended. Her shift never ended, and she never came back, she never even reported to work. His aunt Stacey was a bit abusive; she indulged in sexual perversion. His aunt would beat him, then have him explore her every orifice. At the beginning, Boot felt low and dirty. But as time and years went on he grew into it, and would beg his aunt Stacey to inflict pain on him; in return, he would give her a fucking of a lifetime.

"Come on, baby, get me right," Phatmama said, patting Boot on the thigh and kissing his dick before getting to her feet. Phatmama walked over to her bag; she removed a piece of rope with loops at the ends along with a seven-inch pipe, and a small tube of petroleum jelly. She strapped the vibrating butterfly on her clit and placed the rope around Sherman's neck and slid the pipe through the loops of the rope. "Come on, big daddy!" Phatmama said seductively, waving Boot over.

Boot walked over, still stroking his penis. Phatmama kissed Boot hungrily. He squeezed some petroleum jelly on the tip of his fingers, and he slipped them between the crack and greased her asshole. Then he applied a little to the tip of his rod. His manhood flexed, as he worked the petroleum into the head of his rod.

"When you get up in there, don't play no games," Phatmama said, looking into Boot's eyes.

"I don't intend to," Boot retorted, pushing into Phatmama's backdoor.

"Aagghh!" Phatmama yelled as Boot worked himself in her. Phatmama twisted the pipe that made the rope tighten around Sherman's neck, cutting off his air supply. She turned on her butterfly and it buzzed to life stimulating her clitoris. "Oh shit! Boot, do your thang, daddy, beat them guts."

Boot arched Phatmama's back, and found a nice hard rhythm, his pelvis banging against her red mammoth backside. Phatmama enjoyed the pain that Boot gave her by stretching her backdoor. "Ooooh, Boot!" Phatmama rejoiced, turning the rope tighter on Sherman's neck; he struggled to breath. "Oh shit! Oh shit, harder, Boot, harder, damn it!" Phatmama screamed with her face in a mask of pleasure and pain.

Boot grabbed Phatmama's cheeks, spread them apart, and started giving her the business. He made sure every thrust hit her lower intestines; his meat was eaten and spat back out with every thrust. The blister hurt on his navel, as he flexed his abs when he slammed into Phatmama's dookie shute. The butterfly between Phatmama's legs buzzed against her clit, making her super sensitive; she was on the verge of cuming. She could tell how rapidly Boot was running dick in and out of her that he was almost at his peak.

Also, she turned the pipe to its max; Sherman got to bucking in his chair. Phatmama leaned over and nibbled on his ear. "Die, bitch!" she whispered.

Seeing Phatmama's lips on Sherman's ear enraged Boot; he dug his fingers into Phatmama's butt cheeks, and got to serving her strokes like he had lost his damn mind.

"Aggh!" Phamama groaned.

Boot got on his tiptoes and kept on drilling Phatmama. Blood vessels in Sherman's eyes erupted, as he took his last breath; this event took Phatmama where she needed to go. "Oh shit! I'm cuming," Phatmama announced.

"Me too!" Boot gritted out between thrusts; he released deep in Phatmama's anal the way that she liked him to. Phatmama's body shook agitatedly. Boot stood behind Phatmama, locked in place, still inside of her. Phatmama breathed hard, biting down hard on her bottom lip.

Boot backed out of Phatmama, still holding her cheeks apart; her backdoor sat open like the opening of a Snapple bottle. He was satisfied at his work; he let her cheeks fall together, and went to clean up and get dressed. Phatmama had to finish up before she could join Boot in the shower. She grabbed a razor out her bag and made an incision down the middle of Sherman's nut sack; his testicles were still warm in her hand. She severed his squishy nuts from its sack and placed them in his already open mouth. She admired her handiwork before she went to join Boot in the shower.

Chapter 12

Phatmama laid nestled up against Boot's naked body, she loved how her body molded against the hardness of his body. Sour Diesel lingered in the air from the Backwood he was blowing on, the rain beating against the window. It had started drizzling right before they left the Super 8 on New York Ave., leaving Sherman's body to be found by house-keeping.

Now laying in the confinements of Boot's crib, the event was playing out in his head; he had picked up on a new addiction: sex and murder. Something that the savage ass diva beside him loved too. This wasn't Boot's first time indulging in something like this with Phatmama. Their first time was when they killed Tone. He fucked Phatmama in the ass, while she stabbed Tone with a Rambo-styled knife. It was kinda weird at first, but then something overtook Boot and made him feel what he was doing was so right. He felt more than alive from what torture and pleasure normally does for him. Committing these acts with Phatmama kinda made him feel immortal, but that wasn't the only thing that had Boot's mind pondering tonight. Ever since they killed Cain together, they had mysteriously connected. That same night, they were intimate, but Phatmama wouldn't let Boot enter through her vagina, only in her anus. At the time, Boot was so eager to put a pounding on Phatmama he didn't dispute fucking her ass. Every hood nigga liked that dookie chute every once in a while, so he went with it. But every time after that, it had been in the anus. So it had Boot feeling a certain way. He knew that her pussy didn't stink because he had sniffed and tasted that pussy on a few of their encounters. Boot smoked and listened to the rain hitting the bedroom window. He could tell that Phatmama wasn't fully asleep; he could tell by the flow of her breathing. "Here, Phat," Boot said, handing her the Backwood.

Phatmama raised her head off his chest, giving it a kiss, and taking the burning wood from out of his hand. "I thought your ass was going to sit there and smoke all the bud up with ya deep lung ass!" Phatmama said teasingly.

"Shit! I had to get mine off the top, 'cause you ain't got no small set of lungs on you as you think," Boot stated playfully, scratching Phatmama's scalp with his fingertips.

She loved when he did that to her. "Nigga, whatever!" Phatmama took a pull on the Backwood.

"See, look how that cherry lit up on the Backwood, bringing light in the room. You can only do that if you got some lungs on you."

Phatmama busted out laughing, going into a coughing fit, and punching Boot in his side, which made Boot laugh also. "See, look what you made me do, got me coughing and shit with your playful ass," Phatmama stated, wiping tears from her face, and handing the work back to Boot.

Boot hit the Backwood. "Aye, Phat, let me ask you something?" He had to get his thoughts off his chest, and he didn't see why it couldn't be now.

"Wassup, Boot?" Phatmama asked.

Even though Boot couldn't see Phatmama's face, he knew she was staring at him. "What are we? I mean are we a couple or are we together on some killing and pain and pleasure shit?"

Phatmama's face had crinkled up, from Boot's line of questions. "What you mean, Boot?"

Boot took another hit off the Backwood. "What a nigga trying to say is, I'm feeling you, Phat. I have a connection with you that's unexplainable. I want to know if you on the same page with me."

Phatmama got very quiet. Boot slightly held his breath. He was never the type to put his feelings out there to a female. "Boot, are you asking are we in a relationship?"

"I don't know if that's what you want to call it, but all I know is that whatever title you place on it, I want it, babe," Boot confessed; he found it easy to come clean with Phatmama in the dark. He wondered if it was because he didn't have to look at her, or whether it was her soft skin against his that made him comfortable.

Boot's statement had fucked Phatmama up mentally . "I feel the same way about you, Boot, but you seen me and who I am. I'm fucked up, Boot, I'm too fucked up and savage to be someone's woman—"

"And you think I'm not?" Boot cut Phatmama off. "Look at me, Phat, I'm no better than you, I have them same savage ways," Boot mouthed in the dark, scratching Phatmama's scalp with his fingertips.

Phatmama closed her eyes under his touch. "I know, Boot, but my shit is complicated, you don't even know why I do the things I do, or why I'm the way that I am."

"And even without knowing, Phat, I want you. I told you about the way my aunt abused and molested me, and how I became what I am, you didn't turn your nose up to me or turn your back on me. You still fucked with me in the long way." Boot passed the Backwood to Phatmama.

She declined it. Boot hit it one last time before he stubbed it out in the ashtray that rested next to the bed on the nightstand. Phatmama knew that Boot was right, and she felt that she owed it to him to tell him her darkest secrets. She licked her lips, and let her secrets loose from her memories and lips. "When I was in the military I was raped by my whole platoon. There wasn't anything I could do out there in the middle of Afghanistan. If I killed one of the members in my platoon, I would have ended up spending life in Fort Leavenworth. So I stuck it out and did what I had to do. I'm not saying that I laid down like a dog and let them just have me. I made them fuckers fight me for it every time." Tears flowed out Phatmama's eyes.

Boot couldn't see her tears, but he could feel the moisture splash down on his chest. He continued to scratch her scalp.

"Billie came to the platoon. I was happy that it was another female there. Considering the fact that she was white, I thought that the platoon would prefer her over me, but they didn't. They raped us both. This went on for a few months, but Billie reached out for some help, and she was moved to the medical unit, and I was relocated to a sniper position. That worked for me because I worked alone, but being transferred came with a price. We had to move guns for an unknown source in the military. Things were going good. I was making money and becoming a helluva sniper, until I sold a drug dealer a crate of guns. He later got caught with one of the firearms, and he traded me in for a shorter prison sentence. From then on, I hated the drug dealers; well, the ones that use their drug money and street status to degrade females."

Boot just listened.

"So every time I come across one of that kind, I kill his ass," Phatmama said, laying her head back on Boot's stomach, and throwing her thigh over him, snuggling in tight as if she thought Boot was going to try and get up and leave after hearing her story.

But he didn't; he kissed the crown of her head and asked another question. "Tell me why you only let me penetrate you in the ass?" Boot asked, dropping his hand to her backside and gave it a squeeze.

Phatmama bit down on Boot's nipple, with tears in her eyes. The sensation stirred something in his manhood, and it started to awaken. "I made a promise to myself that the next man I let into my heart, he's going to be the only one to have access to my pussy. He got to cherish it and me because I have been treated like trash because of it." Phatmama sniffed. "I want that person to be my husband."

Damn! Phatmama had dropped a bomb on Boot. He didn't expect her to say what she had, but he could understand where she was coming from. "I feel you, baby, and I understand your need to save yourself, but if you are open to the idea of me being your man I would love to be," Boot stated calmly.

Phatmama straddled Boot and tongued him with passion. After a few moments of the tongue dancing, Phatmama pulled away. "Boot, I'm telling you now don't fuckin' hurt me," Phatmama said seriously.

Boot cupped a handful of Phatmama's booty. "I have no intention to."

Jibril Williams

Chapter 13

Jelli blew over her cup of green tea. She listened to H.E.R. on her Pandora's box in the kitchen. She closed her eyes and she listened to the melodies that escaped from the speaker. Jelli took a sip and let the hot liquid herbs warm her throat. Her thoughts turned to Diego lying upstairs in the guest bedroom. The doctors said that he was going to make it, and thank God that Cain had crooked doctors on his payroll that could handle the situation like the one Diego had gotten himself into yesterday. She had to give it to him, though, the young nigga had mad heart. He just didn't have the brains to go with the heart. Which would cost him months of pain and a shit bag. Jelli turned her nose up, thinking about him defecating in the bag. She was happy that they had a nurse on call because she definitely wasn't going to change his shit bag. When the meds wore off this morning, and she was able to speak to him, all he wanted to know was whether Tata was dead. Jelli couldn't confirm or deny the state of Tata's life, but she informed him that she had made several calls to various different hospitals and to the morgue, and Tata wasn't in any one of them, but that didn't say she did crawl off and die under an abandoned house like some ole stray dog. The thought of that made Jelli smile. Diego begged her to send someone to go check up on Ski and her mother. She was kinda skeptical about having someone go past Tina's apartment due to the fact Tina was the sister of her truest nemesis. But what the fuck! She was feeling like some drama anyway. She was thinking if she killed Tina, then maybe that would draw Tata out if she wasn't already dead. But she would see what today would bring after she checked on the shipment coming in from Weedy. Fate came in the kitchen and stopped in his tracks.

"Damn, that's how you feel this morning?"

"Yup!" Jelli said with a bright smile, taking a bow and steadying the Princess crown on her head. Fate was starting to think the bitch was off her rocker. He didn't understand why Diego would give her the crown off of Zoey's head after he dragged her body through the street. "Don't you think it's about time you got rid of that thing? If the wrong person sees you with that on, it could bring us a lot of heat. The type of heat that this family don't need."

"Hold up, playboy. I say what's best for this family. If I ask for your advice then give it. If I don't, then shut the fuck up!" Jelli spoke with authority in her voice. Fate looked at Jelli like she had four dicks hanging out her mouth. And she looked back at him, like, *Nigga what!*

"Point taken, are you ready?" Fate asked, pushing Jelli's verbal disrespect to the side.

"Yeah, I'm ready," Jelli said, sitting her tea cup in the kitchen sink. Jelli placed the crown on the kitchen table, grabbed her Chanel bag and her Chanel frames, then she was out the door with Fate leading the way. A white 2020 Tahoe sitting on 28's was waiting for them. Jelli hopped in the back, and Fate took his position behind the wheel. Fate peeped in his mirror back at Jelli, as he put his Versace shades on his face. He couldn't help but notice the advertising camel toe that threatened against the crotch of Jelli's black Billionaire jeans. The fitted Billionaire T she wore had her melons pressed firmly against its fabric. Fate smirked to himself. "A fucking she-devil!" he mumbled.

Jelli's phone vibrated with a text from Sparko confirming that he got the package. Shortly after, she got notification from Fatts and Flame saying they all encountered their product. She gave the three men twenty-five bricks apiece. Thirteen bricks of heroin and twelve bricks of Canadian white. Everyone else she gave ten bricks apiece. There was no doubt in her mind that after the performance she put on in their last meeting, she wouldn't have a problem getting her money back. She looked down at the diamond ring that rested on her left hand. The finger next to her pinky. The thought of Cain came to mind. She wondered, was he smiling down on her or was he in heaven sitting on a cloud staring down at her mad as hell? *Don't be mad, bae, you showed me what you showed me for a reason*, Jelli thought to herself.

"Boss lady, how you want to handle the situation with Tata about shooting Diego?" Fate said, breaking Jelli's thoughts. Fate couldn't read Jelli's eyes through her shades. Jelli paused, as if she was searching for the right words to say.

"We wait until the time is right before we crush her and the rest of them bitches. Until then, let's get money."

"You know that's not gonna sit well with Diego hot headed ass!" Fate retorted, looking at Jelli through his rearview.

"Well, hopefully, a bullet to the stomach and a shit bag will cool his ass down until we ready to make our move on Tata," Jelli stated calmly, laying her head on the head rest.

Fate and Jelli pulled up on Mt. Pleasant. They got out in front of a small dry cleaner's—One of Cain's small business fronts and stores that he laundered his drug money through. Fate and Jelli walked to the back, bypassing the older man who worked the counter and ran the dry cleaners. He only acknowledged Jelli and Fate with a nod, and went back to reading his morning paper. The back of the shop was hot and smelled of scratch fabric softener. Jelli sat down in a green plastic chair, and Fate opened the back door to get some air circulating in the room. He stood posted by the door. On the outside of the door there was a black storm door that was equipped with black steel bars. You needed a key to access the door. Fate lit a cigarette. "How long Cain had this place?" Jelli asked, as she looked around the cleaners.

Fate turned around and looked at the overworked dry cleaners. "As long as I can remember, but the beauty of it is, no one would ever think someone would use this place to run a multimillion dollar drug business out of. That was the impeccable thing I loved about Cain. He was a thinker, he had a gift of doing shit in plain sight, and no one ever caught on because he wasn't flamboyant. Real gangstas move in silence." Fate hit the jack and blew smoke out the storm door. Jelli was about to ask another question, but a green chemicals delivery truck pulled out back. Three workers hopped out the truck, wearing gray work jumpers with hats to match the name: *Johnny Cleaning Supplies* was stamped on them. The men quickly started unloading the truck. One posted up against the truck, taking a smoke break, but it was clear that he was the lookout, and the bulge in his jumper told he was packing major heat. The other two workers placed three large barrels on dollies, and brought them to the back door. Fate unlocked it and let them in. No words were exchanged. As soon as the last barrel was brought in, the workers loaded up their dollies, and were gone.

Jelli looked at the barrels. "Is this is supposed to be the product?"

"Yeah."

"This shit looks like fabric softner and detergent to me, Fate."

100

"I told you Cain had a way of doing shit in plain sight." Fate walked over, tilted the barrel; you could see the liquid move around on the barrel. Then he twisted the barrel lid and removed it; he waved Jelli over. Inside the barrel was hollowed out with another tube, and inside the tube sat bricks of heroin and coke.

Jelli smiled to herself and mumbled, "I be damn."

***

Whip stood over Tata, watching her sleep. He leaned over and rubbed his nose against hers; he closed his eyes, taken in by the texture of her skin. "I thought I lost you, bae," Whip whispered, and softly planted a small kiss on Tata's luscious lips. Tata immediately turned head, balling her pretty little face up.

"Humm, huh, ugh! Papi, no kisses, my breath stank right now," Tata mumbled. A Kool-Aid smile came across Whip's face.

"I ain't trying to hear that, woman, I'm good enough to eat ya coochie but I'm not good enough to taste your bad breath?" Whip said, grabbing her face and kissing her deeply. Her breath was kinda tart, but he wasn't going to say anything. He was just happy that he was able to kiss her.

"I feel like shit, Papi." Tata confessed.

"Well, that's what happens when you get shot, but take it easy. You going to be alright."

"My leg is killing me. Them bullets ain't no joke, bae." Tata giggled.

"Shit, you don't have to tell me—I been there before," Whip said, running a finger across Tata's bottom lip.

"Papi, please get me something to drink and my phone, my mouth feels like sand," Tata said, running a dry tongue over her lips.

"Yeah, bae, I got cha." Whip left and came back with a bottle of water and some papaya juice. He helped Tata sit up in bed and helped her consume the fluids. "Damn, bae, slow down—We got plenty of water and juice," Whip stated, as he wiped juice from the side of Tata's face.

"If your ass was as dehydrated as I am, you would be taking big gulps too, Tata retorted, slightly embarrassed.

"It's all good, baby, don't even trip, you still the boss," Whip said.

"Where is everyone?" Tata asked.

"I ran everyone off. As you know, Boot and Phatmama are somewhere together. I don't know what's up with them but they have become glued to the hip outta nowhere. Billie is upstairs taking a nap, and Racks is checking the traps." Whip handed Tata his phone. "We gotta get you a new phone because we found out Diego tracked you through your phone by using an app. So, use mine."

Tata was hesitant at first, but after a brief pause she placed a call to Ra'uf about an agreement they made. That was all Whip could pick up on the one-sided conversation. Tata disconnected the call and handed Whip back his phone.

"Thank you, Whip," Tata said.

"For what?" Whip looked confused.

"For saving me. If it wasn't for you I would have been dead."

"There's no need for praise, Tata. If the tables were turned, I know you would have done it for me." Whip kissed Tata's lips. "But let me tell you how ole boy found you. He tracked you through your phone through some app. Also, Sticks handled that business with Tina and Ski and got the audio recordings. He also recovered the ransom money. Phatmama rewarded him with two hundred and fifty stacks.

102

"Yes!" Tata blurted out. She was relieved that she didn't have them recordings looming over her head and the threat of going back to jail. "I need you to call a meeting, we getting back to the money," Tata said.

"What about Jelli and Diego and the attempt on your life?" Whip asked with concern in his voice.

"We get our money right, then we go to war," Tata said, scooting down on the bed and closing her eyes.

Jibril Williams

Chapter 14

4 months later

"When you came to work this morning, was you prepared to die?" the robber asked the Cartier Jeweler security guard who was trying to reach for his spare piece that he kept in an ankle holster. The guard looked up into the barrel of the robber's Glock 17 with the 30-round extended clip. His eyes then landed on the robber's face which he couldn't clearly see through the plastic face mask the robber wore over her face. The black hijab that covered her head fully only showed a piece of colored hair that stuck out from the right side of her hijab, which matched the red bottoms she wore. In fact, that's how all the robbers in the Cartier Jeweler shop identified each other—by the color of hair that matched their red bottoms. The guard shook his head in fear. "Then why would you do some dumb geeking ass shit that you're trying right now?" the robber wearing her pink red bottoms said, squatting down and removing the hi point .380 from his ankle holster. "You gonna pay for this, papi," the robber said, and then yelled out: "Two minutes!"

Phatmama and Billie worked the display cases; they dumped trays and trays of Cartier's best jewelry in their bags. Phatmama emptied out the Cartier watch collection while Billie hit their ring and tennis bracelet collection. Normally, Phatmama drove the getaway and did the lookout, but they couldn't get Racks strap-on wearing ass into a pair of Red Bottom heels; she bucked so hard against it, and even when Tata finally convinced Racks, the babe couldn't even take three steps without her stumbling and falling. So Racks held the front line down, by being their eyes and their wheels.

"Clear!" Phatmama yelled out.

"Clear!" Billie yelled, confirming that her display case was empty.

Damn them bitches did their thang, Tata thought to herself, seeing that they were finished a minute ahead of schedule. "Alright, little daddy, bring us home," Tata said in her earpiece. Billie backed up to the front entrance, waving her gun over top of the Cartier shoppers. It was funny how Tata had everyone face down ass up in the store. It was waggish to Billie to see the old white lady face down ass up. You could tell her boogie ass never been in this sexual position before in her life.

"Let's roll!" Racks came through Tata's earpiece. Tata had seen the gray sprinter van pull up out the corner of her eye. Tata nodded at Phatmama who was standing behind the counter. Phatmama hit a button that was located on the counter next to the register. The button buzzed the store entrance, unlocking the door so Billie could get out. Billie held the door open for Phatmama, and Phatmama held it open for Tata. Tata stood looking at the Cartier guard; she took aim with her Glock. The guard's ass was in the air. "The next time I come in here, obey my orders." Tata let off a single shot, hitting the guard in his left butt cheek. The guard's scream was louder than the gunshot. She smirked behind her mask and walked out. Phatmama shook her head and followed behind Tata. They got into the sprinter van, and headed towards the D.C. and Maryland line.

***

"What's on your mind, blood? You quiet as a muthafucka. The only time you quiet like this is when splackin a nigga on your mind or something heavy. What is it, blood?" Whip asked.

Boot looked as his blood rode. He was thinking whether or not he wanted to discuss with Whip what was on his mind. He and Whip had been through hell and back over the last few months. Shit had been great for them with the new plug they got. With Tata introducing them to Rau'f, the money been coming by the box load. The Johnny boy's spot had been jumping out the gym with the money. Sticks had the Georgia Ave. trap rocking. The Northeast trap had turned into a gold mine. The new spot in Potomac Gardens and 7th and T-street made the D.C. Bloods see a two hundred thousand profit a week, and they met some bloods down NC that was coming up every two weeks buying two bricks of heroin for 125 apiece. Whip had gotten smart and opened a few CBD ointment and oils shops.

He had his aunt running that aspect of the business, but Whip was looking to invest in more legit businesses. Boot didn't want Whip to think he was switching up on him when things were going so good with building their nation. But they'd been through too much to hold shit from Whip.

Boot reached in his right pocket and removed a small red Tiffany's box and handed it to Whip. "What you think, blood?" Boot asked. Whip pulled up at Tata's new apartment after she was shot by Diego. Whip had her move from her Oakcrest Towers apartment and relocated to Sussex Square apartments out Capitol Heights MD. Whip took the box from Boot and opened it

Whip looked at the 2 ½ red princess cut diamond over that rested exquisitely on a black onyx band. Whip looked at the ring, then at Boot, then back at the ring.

"Damn, Slim, I never thought you viewed me in that light, but I can't marry you—I'm married to the streets and I like pussy," Whip said, smiling.

"Man, fuck ya! You got jokes," Boot said, trying to snatch the ring out of his hand, but Whip quickly moved from his grasp.

"Hold up, who is this for? Phatmama?" Whip asked, looking surprised.

"The one and only!" Boot stated without hesitation.

"Blood, you serious with it, huh? What that crazy ass broad done to my nigga for you to want to marry her? She licked that ass, didn't she?" Whip stated, clowning Boot.

"Nigga, don't nothing get close to my ass hole but toilet paper and shit—I'm a G all the fucking way through!" Boot retorted, throwing up his B's on his hand. "Ain't no fuckin' homo thug here, nigga," Boot added.

Whip cried out with laughter. "Man, I respect your gangsta. That's why I'm curious as to why you want to marry this broad. We getting major money and we got so much more money to make."

"It's complicated, Whip, but what I feel about Phat is like no other. When have you ever seen me boo'd up with a chick?"

Whip thought about it for a minute. He and Boot had been friends over seventeen years, and he couldn't recall him ever having a girlfriend or a woman that he labeled as his woman. "I never saw you with a girlfriend, but that makes me even more concerned, because you talking about marrying Phatmama. What do you know about being a husband? We didn't grow up with fathers and our moms never had a husband, so what do you know about being a husband? A husband is a lifetime partner." Whip handed the Tiffany box back to him. The statement was ponderous to

Boot. He grabbed the box from Whip and stared down at the ring before he closed the lid.

"To be honest, blood, I don't know shit about being a husband. I been a G, a hustler, all my life, but when it comes to Phat, there is no mountain I won't climb for her. There's not an ocean that I won't drown in or swim for her. I would wage war against God for my bitch. Phatmama completes me, bruh."

Whip pushed his bifocals back on his nose as he listened to Boot. Just hearing his man talk like this about Phatmama, he knew Phatmama had her hooks all the way in him. He also knew Boot was a man that does what he wanted and for Boot to be talking to him about his love for Phatmama and marrying her, Boot wanted his blessings and who was he not to give his partner the blessing he needed! "Blood, I honor what you are saying—You have my blessings," Whip said, reaching his hand out so him and Boot could shake it up. "Speaking of the devil herself—There goes your Phat right there," Whip said, as Phatmama whipped her truck into the parking spot next to them. The Red Bottom Squad jumped out of Phatmama's ride, looking dangerous and sexy.

Jibril Williams

Chapter 15

"You muthafuckas have been tearing them cracka's stores up! Goddamn! Look at this shit, Blood," Boot said, amazed at all the merch that was scattered across Tata's living room floor. There wasn't much walking room with all the jewelry that occupied the floor. This was the fourth job the Red Bottom Squad pulled off this month. They wiped the Rolex shop clean out Penguin city. Tiffany's and shops out Georgetown didn't stand a chance. Now Cartier took a major loss today, and last month the Red Bottom Squad hit two banks and came off with two hundred thousand from each bank.

The living room floor was littered with platinum Daytona Oyster masters, white gold Cellini Moonphase, Patek Calatrava, Yacht-Masters, Jaeger-LeCoultre. The floor was covered with every watch probably known to man. The Rolexes and Cartiers were in various different sizes, and in various different colors—from rose gold to pink gold, yellow and white gold—these were just in watches alone; the other half of the living room floor consisted of necklaces, bracelets, rings, and toe rings. The Red Bottom Squad had been getting it in. Ra'uf came through on his end of the deal with giving Tata the financial backing. He bought her a club right off top of Good Hope Road. It used to be a club called *The Legend* back in the days, but Tata had it gutted out and she dropped every dime in her name to get the club back up and running. She had even added some innovation to the club. The club will be opening in one week. Rau'f used his contacts to get a liquor license. Tata had been grinding hard trying to get club Red Bottom open; she'd been interviewing strippers from all over the United States. She'd been viewing Instagram pages, watching videos of strippers from Dallas, Houston, Miami, Atlanta, Oklahoma, and even local strippers. She got twenty strippers coming in to perform during the opening night. She even got D.C. native—Shy Glizzy—to come through and make an appearance. Rau'f wanted Tata's opening night to be a success, so he reached out to a few NBA and NFL players—from Washington Redskins and The Washington Wizards—to come through and support Tata's opening night. The Red Bottom Squad pulled together and got pornstar Layla Red and Trini Calypso to come through opening night and flex. Tata wanted the whole nation's capital to come for her opening night. All the hard work that the Red Bottom Squad had been putting in was to recuperate all the money that they had put in the club and the entertainment. Tata took inventory of the merch. She went through each piece, marking all the jewelry prices down. Racks sat on the bar stool and rolled some loud packs. Phatmama took up a spot on the couch with her foot up under her, sipping on some Henny, impatiently waiting for Racks to finish twisting up the Backwood. Boot sat next to her, openly rubbing her thigh. Whip watched Tata bend over the merch. Tata was making her estimation down; the black leggings she wore were eaten up by her ass cheeks. Whip's dick jumped in his black Polo jeans every time she would bend down in front of him. He caught a view down her shirt, and her smooth chocolate covered breasts made his mouth water. Tata had recovered well after being shot. She bounced back like nothing happened, and Whip was happy about that, but he was getting frustrated with Tata over the last two months. She hadn't paid him much attention. If she wasn't plotting or pulling off a heist, she was knee-deep with matters dealing with the club. The only thing that was good over the last few months was the plug

Tata introduced him to. He was now getting each key from Rau'f at fifty bands apiece. The only thing was, he hadn't met Rau'f yet, and everything had to go through Tata until further notice. But other than that, Tata had only been intimate with him three times since the shooting. And he was getting ready to step out on Tata if he couldn't get any loving from her.

Tata could feel Whip's eyes barreling through her. She could feel the tension building up in him, and she knew that Whip needed some intimate time with her. Tata respected Whip for not crowding her and demanding her time, but right now she was on a mission to get that bag. She didn't want to be robbing jewelry stores forever. She knew that wasn't going to last forever, and depending on a nigga was out the question. Tata knew she loved Whip; she had to let him know that soon, or she was gonna lose him.

"Is Sticks gonna to be at the club when it opens?" Billie asked out the blue. The room fell silent.

"Why you asking about Sticks?" Tata asked, putting her inventory to a halt.

"I just wanted to know. Damn, is it a Red Bottom sin to ask about a man?" Billie said bashfully, not looking at Tata.

"Naw, hell naw, you got a thing for Sticks, don't cha?" Phatmama chimed in. Billie blushed hard, turning her creamy white skin pink. Billie didn't know why she didn't ask Racks about Sticks; after all, Sticks was a blood just like Racks. Besides, she knew she would have gotten a better response outta Racks than Phatmama or Tata.

"I don't really know if I got a thing for him or not—I haven't seen him around but twice since Tata got shot, but he does look interesting!" Billie admitted.

"You want to suck that dick, don't you?" Tata said, busting out laughing. Boot had to laugh with Tata on that.

"Man, leave Billie alone—That's not how you treat a person who saved my baby life," Whip interrupted the group's horse play.

"Every member of D.C.B will be at the club opening—Matter of fact, let me see your phone for a minute," Whip said, tiptoeing through the merch that was on the floor. Billie handed Whip her phone. Whip dialed Sticks' number. He picked up on the second ring

"Who this?" Sticks' voice shot through the phone.

"It's Whip, blood, I got someone here that wants to speak with you." Whip handed Billie her phone back. Billie turned a shade pinker. All eyes were on her; she snatched the phone from Whip and ran down the hallway of Tata's apartment like a teenage girl who had a crush on the boy next door. Everyone broke out in laughter at Billie antics.

"I bet she be sending him pussy pix by the end of the night," Phatmama said, laughing.

"Leave that girl alone, Phatmama." Tata was grateful that they had brought Billie on board the Red Bottom Squad. Billie had been a helluva asset to the team. Tata looked over towards Racks. Racks hadn't been the same since Zoey died; she missed Zoey. The whole team did. Tata made a mental note to have a sit-down with Racks after the club opening. Tata started loading a bag up with merch. She had a few hours to kill before she met up with Rau'f to trade the goods in for cash. She needed a shower, and she needed to handle some business with Whip. Tata loaded two bags up and sat them next to the couch where Boot and Phatmama were boo'd up.

She walked over to Whip, who was smoking a Backwoods that Racks had rolled. Tata grabbed his face and put her forehead against his. "Hey, papi."

The gesture kinda caught Whip off guard. Smoke seeped out of Whip's mouth as he responded: "What it do?" Tata wrapped her juicy lips on Whip's bottom lip, and sucked on it rapidly; a tingle started to formulate in his manhood. He sucked back on Tata's luscious lips, gripping a handful of her backside with his left hand. His hand sunk into her plumpness. Phatmama threw a hand over Boot's eyes so he couldn't see the show that Whip and Tata were putting on.

"Ummm, excuse me, freaks! Don't forget that you fuckers got company," Phatmama said, making Tata laugh with Whip's tongue in her mouth. Tata led Whip off to the bedroom after he passed the Backwood to Boot. Whip smacked Tata on the ass, as she led him down the hall towards the bedroom. She put her stank walk on—You know that walk that all project chicks learn how to do; that walk that all hood niggas love to watch a woman walk. Whip loved when Tata walked like that, especially for his pleasure.

"Papi, I need to apologize to you—I know that I been neglecting, and I'm sorry, but with losing Zoey and trying to keep the squad fed, getting shot and trying to open a legit business, I kinda lost focus on you."

"Shh! Whip held his finger up to her lips, silencing Tata. "Baby, I don't want to hear nothing about the club right now, babe. I just want to enjoy you for the moment."

"Say no more," Tata said, leading Whip to the bed. She took a seat at the foot of the bed, keeping Whip in front of her. She unbuckled his Gucci belt, and unbuttoned his jeans. Tata worked his jeans and boxer briefs around his ankles while she made intense eye contact.

Tata held his half erect manhood. She had every intention to suck his dick like a true savage bitch; she stroked him while she kissed and sucked on his thighs. Whip grew stiffer in her small soft hands. Tata lifted up his nuts, buried her face up under them, and inhaled deeply. She loved Whip's natural scent. It was like an aphrodisiac. She dropped Whip's nuts in her mouth.

"Aaah!" Whip let out a sound of pleasure.

Tata pushed Whip's man plums around in her mouth with her tongue, soaking them with her saliva. She continued to slow-stroke Whip. She was waiting for the right time to put him in her mouth. She brought Whip's nuts out her mouth with a suction sound. Whip's nuts shone with Tata's saliva. Tata started kissing and sucking Whip's other thigh, still making eye contact with Whip. She skinned Whip all the way back to his base, and gave his manhood a tight squeeze, slightly shaking him in her hand; this made Whip's manhood swell to the hilt. She knew Whip was ready, but she wasn't ready. Tata spat on Whip's palpitating dick and used the spit to lube him. Tata jacked Whip.

"Oh shit!" Whip said, standing on tiptoe.

"You like that, papi?" Tata asked, as she jacked him.

"Uhmm," was all Whip could say, and that's all Tata needed to hear. She aggressively popped Whip's dick in her mouth, and started sucking that joker like there was no tomorrow. She moved her head from side to side, making all kinds of sucking noises with it. She popped him in and out in the back of her throat. He responded to Tata's tactics by slightly thrusting his pelvis into her mouth, making Tata gag. Spit shot out from around Whip's dick, but Tata kept working her magic on his magic stick. Tata came off the dick, breathing hard. She patted his hammer against her luscious lips.

"You gonna nut in my face, papi. You gonna give mami that nut, huh?" Tata said in her begging voice

"Yeah, bae, let's do that shit!" Whip anxiously replied

Tata was back in action with Whip in her mouth; she had a steady bob going on. Whip was on tiptoe, with both hands on top of Tata's head. He was really fucking her face now. Tata had to put a hand on his thighs to take the edge off his thrust. With every stroke Whip made, the tip of him tapped the back of Tata's throat. His manhood began to spasm. He wanted to pull out and splash Tata's face with his seed, but Tata's throat clasped his dick. When she un-clenched his dick, she playfully shoved him backwards, causing Whip to fall on the bed with a light coat of sweat on his forehead. Whip was trying to catch his breath. "I don't know what you breathing hard for, papi, I haven't even got-ten mine yet," Tata said, coming out her leggings and shirt, and crawling on top of Whip.

Jibril Williams

Chapter 16

The clouds of smoke lingered in the air of his bedroom. The room had an eerie feeling, as if death was looming over him. Diego didn't give a fuck. He felt like everything that he had to live for was gone. He sipped from the bottle of Hennessy, as he swiped pics across his phone of his uncle: Cain, and his girlfriend—Ski. He missed them both. *How could them muthafucka's kill an angel like Ski*, Diego thought to himself. He stopped at a pic on his phone—him and Ski were together lying in bed with their heads together, throwing up the deuce sign. Diego smiled at how beautiful Ski was. A sadness came over him; he felt that he let Ski down. He felt that he was a pariah for doing so. After he was shot four months ago, he had Jelli send someone to check up on Ski and her mother. When Jelli's people got there, they found the door unlocked, and Ski was dead with her head bashed in. They also found her mother dead in the kitchen, holding a newborn baby. The incident had been all over the news. The police were looking for Diego for questioning, as a person of interest. Diego couldn't go talk to the police to clear his name because he was recovering from an undocumented gunshot wound that left him with a colostomy bag. Silver Spring Maryland Police Department had placed a warrant out for his arrest, and a fifteen-thousand-dollar reward for anyone that could give the authorities any information as to the whereabouts of Diego Ross. So, Fate had Diego sitting on ice until he was able to figure some shit out. Right now, Diego was held up in a cabin that one of Fate's old flames owned in N.C. Diego swiped his phone screen, and another pic of Ski appeared. It was a sexy pic of her in a lace Victoria Secret trim thong panty, in his favorite position—Face down, ass up. He smiled at the pic. Diego remembered that he and Ski had made a few videos, and he had them on his phone. He swiped through the phone and found what he was looking for. The video was of Ski giving him fellatio inside of his Lexus. He bit down on his bottom lip, thinking about how gifted Ski was in giving head, and how blessed he was to experience that gift. Diego's manhood started to grow while watching the video. He eased his hand in his sweat pants and stroked himself. The crunching and light scent of the colostomy bag that was located at the bottom of his stomach made him instantly get soft, and anger overtook him. He had to get the fuck outta this cabin and get back to D.C., and get back to the action. Taking Ski and Cain's death lying down was something he wasn't going for. Fate had him stuck out in a cabin with a nurse, and the old broad didn't have a car or anything. Every week, Fate would have supplies sent to them. Fate had erased all his contacts in his phone, and had his number changed. There was no one that he could call, and no one had his new number to call him.

Diego was frustrated to the max. He was thinking about going downstairs in the kitchen and murdering the old broad, and he thought of calling Fate and demanding that he come to get him. He thought against both ideas. Diego scratched his full beard and ran his hand through his small nappy afro. Four months without properly being groomed had him looking like a different person. That clean-cut pretty boy Diego was hidden behind the wool of hair that he had on his face and head. "Think, D, think!" Diego talked to himself, trying to figure out how he was going to get back to D.C. He looked down at his phone, and the picture of him and Ski stared back at him, and a light bulb came on in his head. Diego went to Instagram and accessed his IG account; with a touch of a finger, he was back in touch with the rest of the world. Diego was getting hyped, strolling through the pictures on the gram. He went and found someone that he could trust. He sent Sess a message to his DM: *"AYE SLIM SHOOT ME UR # ASAP!"* Sess must have been already on the gram fucking with some hoes or something, because when Diego laid his phone down to go take a piss, he got a notification that he had a message from Sess: *"hit me on IMO @sessdabest.*

Diego was familiar with the app, so he quickly downloaded the app and hit Sess. The phone rang, and Diego's screen went black until Sess's pimpled face invaded the screen of the phone.

"My nigga, what's good?" Sess said, smiling.

"Man, I need you' in the worst way," Diego said in desperation.

"Holla at me, you know I rock with you the long way.

***

"I never knew counting money could ever be a tiresome job," Jelli stated, placing another stack of bills in the money counter, and grabbed another stack of bills, then started a hand count. The way she stood on the other side of the table with a Backwood dangling from the corner of her mouth, while counting money was a beautiful sight, and she was doing all of that with a pair of white booty shorts on.

Jelli turned her head to see if Fate had heard what she had said. She caught Fate in a reverie with lust in his eyes "Fate!" Jelli yelled, bringing Fate out of his daydream.

"Yeah, boss lady." Fate said, removing money from his counting machine.

"I said that I never knew how tiresome counting money could be."

"It's always gonna be a job when you live a life where the money is illegal and you can't trust a soul but yourself to count it." Fate stated in a serious tone. "But just letting you know now, boss lady, some strange shit is going on," Fate stated, changing the subject.

"What you mean *strange*? I thought everyone had turned their money in."

"Everyone did make their drop on time, but with the new clientele we got with the dudes from Ohio and Chi-Town, our product should be shorter. It's like we didn't even pick up new clientele."

"So what are you trying to say, Fate? 'Cause from what I have been seeing, business been good, and it's been damn good!" Jelli said with emphasis. She was feeling like Fate was coming at her as though she couldn't hold shit down because she was a woman, and Fate picked up on that.

"No, boss lady, I'm not attacking your ability to be boss and you right—You are running shit damn good. All I'm saying is that somebody else in this city is making some major moves, and it seems we are starting to feel the effects of it money wise."

What Fate was explaining to her was starting to settle in. "So how much money you think we are short?" Jelli asked.

Fate let out a sigh. "About two or three million," Fate stated. Jelli's eyes popped out her head

"Damn, that's a lot of paper."

"I know, so what are we gonna to do about it?" Fate asked. Jelli knew that Fate was now testing her ability to lead. Her response would make all the difference to her status as boss. Jelli paused and thought for a minute.

"Right now we do nothing. We put our feelers out there, find out who's selling the dope, then we find out who their suppliers are, and we annihilate them."

Fate stood to his feet and started clapping his hands. "Well fucking said. No need to kill the worker when the suppliers are still holding the work; all they gonna do is find more workers."

Jelli lit her Backwood and sat on the table; her shorts cut into her lady box and defined her print. Fate couldn't help but look at Jelli. He knew that he was wrong for looking at Jelli in this manner. Cain was his friend and Jelli was his wifey, but it was that mustard seed in the back of his head that was, like, *Shit, someone gonna fuck her, why not me?* Fate felt like Jelli had some attraction towards him because she caught him admiring her body a few times, but never called him out on it.

"How much we counted so far?" Fate asked. Jelli leaned back on the table and grabbed her phone. The movement made Jelli open her legs up wider, giving Fate the perfect view. His hand dropped down to his crotch and he squeezed himself.

"We are a little over three million, half of that is Weedy money."

"Okay well let's get the rest of this bread counted so we can pay our workers and get some rest."

Jelli made a mental note on how Fate said 'our workers'. She didn't check him because she knew the true colors on a snake would show. She would be waiting when they do. Jelli got off the table and pulled her shorts out the confinements of her crease "Fate, I want to do something for our team to show them our appreciation for them. What you think about that?"

"That's boss shit, show love and they'll love you back. What you got in mind, Jelli?

"I don't know right now, but I would let you know when I come up with something," Jelli said, reloading the counting machine.

Chapter 17

Racks fingered the .223 bullet with its red tracers tip. She sat low in her white Lexus RX 450h with a smoke-gray complexion and sitting on smoke-gray 26-inch Diablo rims. This was a big step up from her Delta 88.

D.C.B. business has been good for her and the team; they were all eating, but Racks wasn't fazed by the money. She only purchased the SUV because everyone else was grabbing new whips, and she wanted to keep up the assumption that she was okay with the movement, but deep down inside she wasn't. Racks lost her cousin—Gunz—to the game; even though the person who caused his death was now non-existent, the wound of losing him never fully healed. Then Zoey got murdered, and that wound reopened, and her pain was renewed. At first, everyone felt Zoey's death, but then the money started coming in, and everyone seemed to have forgotten about Zoey. But she couldn't erase Zoey from her memory. Zoey was everywhere she looked. She'd seen Zoey in a stranger's smile or the gleam in their eye. Even the sight of a teenager the other day sucking on a blow pop brought back memories of Zoey. She walked into her bedroom last week, and she swore she smelt a hint of Zoey's favorite fragrance—*Love Spell* body spray. She spent a whole hour in her room trying to catch a whiff of Zoey. What enraged Racks was the fact that even after they murdered Zoey, they kidnapped her corpse and dragged her body through the streets like a dog, like she was a piece of shit.

Racks' heart was heavy; her eyes were bloodshot and bone-dry because she'd cried her soul out. She didn't have another ounce of tears in her; all she had to offer was revenge. She'd been through the city on the low, trying to get a line on Jelli, but without driving some type of suspicion to herself. She hadn't been successful with her solo mission, but she vowed that once the first chance to hit Jelli presented itself, she was going to take it. She didn't give a fuck what Whip or Tata said. Racks watched Tata come out the Lexus dealership pulling a Louis Vuitton rolling suitcase. Racks started the Lexus, and hit the unlock latch button on the door.

Tata opened the back passenger door and hoisted the suitcase in the back seat. It was almost a struggle for her, but she got it. Racks thought for a moment that she was gonna have to get out and help her. Tata jumped in the passenger seat, put her Glock between her legs, and strapped herself in with the seatbelt.

"You got some bud on ya, Racks?—A diva needs a blunt or something," Tata said.

"Naw, I left everything I had on me at your spot. We can swing by one of the spots and pick something up to blow."

"No, we got to take this money straight to the crib so I can count it up and break bread. Then I gotta shoot by the club. I'm not trying to get stopped on the south side with all this bread on me. It's gonna be real hard to explain how and where I got two mill from."

"Damn! Two million, huh? I see that Rau'f came through for us as always."

"Rau'f is a true businessman—He gets a little flirty at times, but that come with the game—He wouldn't be a man if he didn't," Tata replied. She had asked Racks to accompany her for a reason. She'd been doing business with Rau'f long enough now to trust him and come alone. Tata wanted to talk with Racks about her being distant since the death of

Zoey. She wanted to let Racks know that she was there if she needed anything. Tata didn't know how she was going to approach the situation, so she just went at it. "I miss her too, Racks," Tata abruptly stated.

"Miss *who*?" Racks retorted, being caught off guard by Tata's statement.

"Zoey! I miss her."

"I never said you didn't," Racks replied. The vibe in the SUV became awkward for Racks.

"No one said you did, but I have two eyes, Racks, and I been watching and I've notice that you have been withdrawn since Zoey died."

"No—Since she was murdered, Tata! She didn't just die, she was murdered!" Racks stated aggressively. Tata could see that Racks had been really holding this in, but she wasn't going to let her go on her like that.

"I know she was killed—I was there, Racks—I was the one that closed her lifeless eyes," Tata stated with tears welling up in her eyes. "Where all this anger coming from towards me?" Tata inquired.

Racks let out a deep sigh, and pulled the SUV into traffic. "Tata, I don't have an issue with you. My issue is with everyone. I just feel that we letting them get away with killing Zoey."

"What! I would never let them get away with what they did to Zoey. Jelli is gonna get what's coming to her. I'm never letting this shit go." Tata wasn't comfy that Racks was thinking that she was brushing Zoey's death to the side.

"But damn, it's been almost seven months and we haven't sent one single bullet Jelli way, or applied any type of pressure her way."

"And that's done by design and strategy. Listen, Racks, over the last few months, a lot of shit been happening.

Muthafuckas dying on both sides. An undercover agent gets murdered in a jewelry heist which my boyfriend Rico was involved in. The Red Bottom Squad murdered Rico, shit being jumping off with the D.C.B's. I heard about that shit that happen out Johnny Boys and the nigga Spoon getting killed, and we can't forget about Ink, Cee and Tone. Then the city had the biggest shoot-out of all time at Club Bass & Cru that left Zoey and Cain dead. And we definitely can't forget about the aftermath of their killings that bleed over into their funerals. All that's been happening in the city, Racks, we been tied into it someway." Tata frowned as she broke shit down to Racks' ass; she really needed a smoke now.

"But I hear ya—"

"No, you don't hear me, Racks, because you gearing up to rebutt me on what I said. We been getting away with a lot of shit. Them crackas got investigations going on, and we need to steer clear of hot drama, let this shit blow over, make this money in the meantime and once everything is calm, we get back on our oars and bring Jelli hell."

Racks understood what Tata was dropping on her. She respected what she was saying, but she was a person of action. Racks couldn't start something and not finish it. Sometimes this trait was a gift, but at times it was a curse. Racks couldn't let Tata know this, so she just agreed to keep from disagreeing. "You know what? You dead ass right. I'm wrong, I'm moving off my emotions. Thanks for having this talk with me." Racks stuck her hand out, so her and Tata could shake it up.

"It's all good, Racks, just know that we in this shit together and we will give Jelli her muthafuckin share of death," Tata said, then placed her head on the head rest and closed her eyes.

***

"I don't give a fuck! I didn't drive nine fuckin' hours for free. I'm not no fuckin' Uber driver! You gonna give me some dick, Diego!"

"Come on, Fanny, you tripping like clown shoes. Sess is your baby dad, and that's my nigga."

"Man, fuck Sess bumpy face ass—He's not fucking me right, anyway—He tends to out there in them streets distributing that community dick between his legs," Fanny said with hostility in her voice.

"So what! You not distributing community pussy right now?" Diego fired back in his man's defense.

"Boy, stop! There's nothing community about my pussy! My pussy is clean and it's *good too*!" Fanny said proudly, popping her lips.

Diego looked at the chocolate bitch with the blue colored hair. Fanny was fine as hell, but she was your everyday woodland project chick. Diego looked down at Fanny's thighs and how her shaved pussy was peeking out the bottom of her one-piece fitted Prada dress. The more Fanny moved her legs, the more her dress inched up, and the more of her love box could be seen.

Fanny followed his eyes, and she knew she had him. "Come on, Diego, what you gonna do? A bitch horny as fuck, and I got a long drive back to D.C. Are you riding with me or not?" Fanny reached over and grabbed Diego's dick through his sweatpants.

Diego hated that he let Sess talk him into letting his baby mama come to pick him up. He hated more that his dick was swelling under Fanny's touch. Fate had slipped and ordered Diego some clothes online. When the packages came, they had the cabin address on them. So he shot Sess the address, and that's how Fanny ended there begging for the dick.

"Come on, Fanny, this shit ain't cool. What you doing?" Diego was trying to talk some sense into Sess's baby mama.

"I can't tell it's not cool, *big fella* right here seems to think it's alright," Fanny retorted, skillfully going in Diego's sweatpants, releasing his meat from its confinements. Diego didn't do anything to stop her; his eyes went back to her shaved pussy, then back to his dick. Every time Fanny would stroke him, precum would ooze from his dick. He released and pushed the Kia car seat all the way back until the seat couldn't go back any farther. Diego worked his sweats over his hips and down to his Jordan 3's.

"Come on, bitch let's get it!" Diego said.

Fanny pulled her dress over her head, exposing her naked body. She straddled Diego in the car seat. Fanny didn't even comment on his colostomy bag; her mind was on getting the dick. She'd been longing to fuck Diego for a long time. "Where the rubber at, Fanny?" Diego asked.

"Uhn Uhn! Raw, dog," Fanny whispered, swiping the head of Diego's manhood between her creases, before she eased him inside of her.

Chapter 18

Nightfall just came over D.C. when Fanny and Diego had reached the city. Diego was pissed at Fanny's thot ass for the stunt she pulled. Every two or three hours during the drive back from N.C., she demanded that Diego beat the pussy up; if not, she wouldn't drive a mile farther. Diego was at the nympho's mercy. Diego wasn't too disappointed though after his second orgasm. Fanny had a nice piece of pussy on her that Diego had no complaints about. During the drive back, if they weren't fucking, Fanny was talking. Diego learned that she was somewhat a hood celebrity with doing manicures and pedicures. The girl had mad talent. Fanny showed him her IG page. Shawty had 300,000 followers. Diego couldn't even lie; Fanny's work was the best that he had ever seen. He had wondered why she hadn't opened her own shop and branded her talent.

Fanny also filled him in on the gossip about him killing his girlfriend and her mother. The city was filled with rumors that he killed Ski and Tina because they had stolen some money from him. The authorities had come to that conclusion because they received a tip from crime stoppers. Diego's head was spinning from all the shit Fanny told him. The most disturbing news about the rumors, after reviewing the whole news feed on Fanny's phone, was that after he killed Tina, he left Tina's new born son sucking on his dead mother's breast.

Diego learned that they had every government agency looking for him. In addition, they had increased the reward money up to thirty thousand dollars. When Diego found out about them upping the reward money, he started looking at

Fanny leading him into a trap. He knew first-hand how money recklessly breeds greed and shadiness. He brushed it off since they had been in the city for thirty minutes now and 'twelve' hadn't gotten on their line yet.

Fanny pulled her Kia to a stop on P Street—off of Good Hope Rd., SE—in front of a white house with a wooden fence around it. Two angry looking pitbulls patrolled the yard. The house had one of them man-made driveways that led to the backyard. "Wait here, Fanny, I'll be right back," Diego said, climbing out of the car.

Diego walked to the gate, and the pits went off. The fence was so flimsy Diego had to take two steps back because he was thinking the fence wasn't going to hold the pits binging against it. The porch light came on, and Mr. Bill stepped out the house with a hand cannon in his hand.

"Who the fuck is that?" Mr. Bill yelled from the porch

"It's me—Diego!"

"Oh shit! Penny and Dollar, on the porch!" Mr. Bill commanded his dogs. The dogs humbly followed their master's orders. Diego walked through the gate. Mr. Bill met Diego at the bottom of the porch steps and embraced him. "I'm sorry about Cain."

"Me too!" Diego said sadly. "I came to get my survival kit."

"I know you all over the news, Diego, what the fuck happen?" Mr. Bill asked.

"OG, I don't even know and that's real talk."

"Come on, Diego, let's get you going!" Mr. Bill led Diego to the backyard, where a car sat in the middle of the yard with a covering over it. Mr. Bill handed Diego a set of keys while he pulled the cover off the car. A black Chrysler 300 was revealed sitting on factory rims with thirty-five percent tints on it. Diego opened the car door and started the whip.

The engine roared to life with no problem. Diego turned the windshield wipers on, and tapped the brakes four times, and the dashboard opened up. The stash spot held two .45 calibre guns. Diego pulled one from the compartments, and checked the clip, then chambered a round in the head. He hit the latch to pop the trunk of the Chrysler 300; an army-green duffle laid there with a bullet-proof vest. Diego opened the duffle and blue-green bills stared back at him. He was glad that he had listened to Cain's schooling. His uncle told him that every real hustler needs a survival kit in case shit goes wrong, and your survival kit consists of a set of wheels, a few guns, and a bag of money. Also, the kit needed to be laced with fake IDs and names and numbers of the best lawyers in the Metropolitan area. Diego threw about ten bands in his pocket, closed the truck, and hopped behind the wheel.

Mr. Bill came to the driver's window. "I'm gonna get the gate for you."

"Alright, but here—" Diego handed Mr. Bill a handful of bills.

"Naw, Diego, you good—I'm straight—You already taken care of me by helping me keep my house," Mr. Bill said as he went to open the gate.

Diego pulled the 300 out the yard, and waved Fanny on to follow him. Fanny trailed Diego to the gas station on Good Hope Road. Diego parked in the far end of the gas station. Fanny got in the car with Diego, and closed the door. Something about Fanny felt off. Diego looked at her, then out into the gas station lot; everything looked normal. Diego pulled out a stack of money and counted off thirty five hundred, and handed it to Fanny. For a second she seemed as though she didn't want to accept the money, but the project chick inside of her wouldn't allow her not to.

"Diego, can I say something without you getting mad?" Fanny asked, placing the money in her Gucci bag.

"What you got on your mind, Slim?" Diego stated, getting irritated.

Fanny paused, getting her thoughts and courage together "Uhum, I don't think you should trust Sess the way you are doing!" This made Diego's ears prick.

"Why would you say some shit like that? Ain't Sess your baby daddy? Fanny, Sess is my fucking nigga."

"Never mind, Diego, just forget it." Fanny reached for the door handle to exit the car.

"Fuck that, speak on it. You shouldn't have brought it up." Creases invaded Diego's forehead. Fanny was reluctant to finish what she started.

"Sess might be your nigga, but he's my man also. The difference is, I lay down with that nigga. I pillow-talk with your nigga. Diego, I know him better than you would ever know him. You might think that Sess is official, but it's facts that nigga is some type of grimy the worse of the worse. All I'm saying is, don't let him know all your moves." Fanny leaned over, kissed Diego on the cheek, and exited the car.

***

"Shh! Now, no need to cry. This the cost when you out there living the life stuntin' on bitches. You pulled up on me in you Jag and tried to holla. I told you I had a nigga and you told me what my nigga gots to do with you. I denied your advances, and you went on to tell me that you could give me the world, and I took you up on your offer." Phat-mama said those words as she stared down at the man that was strapped to the bed with a gag ball in his mouth. Phat-mama was coming out the hair salon from getting her hair done when this wack ass nigga approached her in the parking lot, trying to holla at her. What made Phatmama mad was, he had just dropped his girl off at the same salon she just came from. So the stranger placed himself in this predicament. After Phatmama denied all his advances, the stranger still didn't back down. When he stated that he could give her the world, Phatmama asked a simple question. "What do I have to do for you to give me the world?"

And the bold muthafucka came out his garbage ass mouth: "Just give a nigga some pussy." Those six words activated the savage within her.

The man struggled within his restraints.

"You never thought to give me the world. You would have to give me your life, huh?" Phatmama placed a leg up on the bed and started rubbing her forefinger over the soft flesh of her clit. You could hear her juices smack and pop when she slid her fingers through the lips of her love box. Phatmama took a pause to take a sip of her glass of wine. Sex, alcohol and murder made her cum the hardest. Phatmama grabbed the knife from the foot of the bed. She slit the man's throat with ease. As he choked on his own blood and bled out like a pig, Phatmama stimulated her clitoris, bringing herself to an orgasm.

"Dad! What the fuck you got going on, dad?" the teenage girl said, walking into the room, scaring Phatmama half to death. Phatmama dropped the wine glass. The scene the girl saw made her believe she caught her dad cheating on her mother. And she was mad. She charged at Phatmama, but Phatmama was skilled in combat. Phat swiftly scooped the knife off the bed, planted it in the girl's stomach, and pushed it downward and twisted it. The girl couldn't have been no more than fifteen years old. Phatmama held the girl's body close to her until the life drained out of her, be-fore she let her fall to the floor. By this time the dad had already expired. Phatmama was still in panic mode, though. She quickly severed the man's limp penis and tossed it on his hairy chest. Phatmama put her clothes on and cleaned up the best she could. She was so much in a rush to get outta there, she could hardly clean up the broken wine glass from the floor.

Chapter 19

"Oh my god! Tata, I can't believe this used to be The Legend. *The Legend* was a nightclub that all D.C. finest hustlers you could think of occupied back in the late 90's. The club drew too many patrons after the Bass & Cru club shooting. "Club Red Bottomz gonna be the hottest gentlemen's club in the city—Look what you have done to this place," Billie stated excitedly, bouncing up and down in Tata's passenger seat, clapping her hands like she was an overly excited child.

"This ain't shit, wait until you see the inside," Tata boasted, killing the engine on her Porsche truck. The truck was an extended gift from Rau'f for fulfilling the contract on Cain's life. The truck was black with pink guts sitting sexy on pink star rims. When Rau'f first presented her with the truck, she didn't like it until Whip told her that the truck reminded him of her because she was dark on the outside and pink in the middle. Tata was tickled how Whip referred the truck to her pussy.

Tata unlocked the mahogany doors to the club, and deactivated the club alarm system. When Tata hit the lights, Billie's mouth dropped. The black walls had red flakes in its paint. The bar was to the right, and black with red trimmings that had the words: *Red Bottomz* written in sexy cursive gold letters. The bar was stocked and ready to go. The club held two stages. One sat in the middle of the floor for the club's main performers, and the other one sat off to the left of it. Both stages were made of highly polished black granite with black alabaster stone. The ceiling had fiber optic lighting that gave you a spacious feeling. The carpet was black and red.

"What yo' bitches in here doing?" Phatmama said, walking in the club with Racks.

"Getting ready for tomorrow's big event," Tata said, walking behind the bar, and poking a bottle of Ace of Spades.

"Why you got the door all open to the club like we don't got beef in these streets?" Phatmama said seriously. Tata couldn't even lie, she was slipping bad.

"You right, Phatmama, I'll tighten up," Tata said, pouring herself some bubbly. Phatmama didn't want to press too hard, so she let Tata off the hook.

"Racks, Phatmama, do you see this place?" Billie stated.

Phatmama started laughing. "Girl, I was the same way when I first saw the club."

"Man, club Red Bottomz is on point, but you need to see the entertainment that me and Phat just picked up from the airport—I swear them bitches gonna leave D.C. rich and the niggas here broke!" Racks said, grabbing her invisible dick through her pants. The group busted out laughing at Racks.

"But look, I want to show you these," Tata said waving the group over to the bar. She pulled out a deck of cards with *Red Bottom* printed on the back of the deck. The deck of cards only held Jacks, Queen, Kings, and Ace's. Tata put one card each on the counter.

"Jacks equals hand jobs at two hundred dollars, Queen equals head only at five hundred dollars, Kings equals pussy at a thousand dollars, and Aces equals the whole shebang—head, pussy and ass for an hour at fifteen."

Billie balled her face up. "Mami, you trying to be a pimp now."

"Hell no, but I know these bitches are going to be trying to run that check up and when a nigga gets drunk in a room full of naked bitches, they gonna want to fuck, so why not capitalize off it?" Tata stated with a look in her eyes, like, *Bitch don't judge me.*

"So where all the fucking going to go down at?" Racks asked.

"In the new wing of the club. The six small private room I had built as an addition to the club. This how it works— Phatmama and me will have the cards. The niggas will buy the card from us, and in return every stripper that has a Red Bottom wrist band on is open to service them. They give the stripper the card. According to which card the customer give them, they would know what type of service to give the customers."

"So you saying if I buy a Queen from you and then I give it to the stripper she will take me to the private room and give me head without question asked?" Racks said, trying to get clarification.

"Bingo!" Tata said. "And the strippers are already on board," she added.

"So how do the strippers get paid?" Billie wanted to know.

"At the end of the night they will bring me or Phat their collected cards and we pay them according to the card after we subtract our cut," Tata stated.

"Well, I be damn, genius!" Billie declared, picking up the bottle of Ace of Spades and taking a long sip.

***

Diego sat on MLK Ave SE. The weight of his .45 rested in his lap. He played his mirrors heavy. An hour after he departed from Fanny, she and Sess had been blowing his phone up. Sess had been trying to get a location on him. Fanny had been texting him, telling him how Sess lost his mind when she pulled up at the crib, and he wasn't with her.

Sess wanted to know where Diego was, what he was driving, what the convo was between them on the way back to D.C. Diego wasn't answering none of their texts until he got a picture of Fanny with a fat lip. She put in the caption: "This is what I get for not giving him any info on you." Diego hit Fanny and told her to meet him on MLK. He saw her Kia drive past him. He told her to park at the end of the avenue and walk back up. Fanny wore a pair of jeans and red shirt that said: *I got good brains*

Diego honked the horn, gaining Fanny's attention. She gave Diego a slight smile and jumped in the car with him.

"Where that nigga at?" Diego asked once Fanny got comfortable in his car, and pulled away from the curb. Fanny tossed a bunch of bags in the back seat.

"He at his apartment. I waited until he went in the bathroom to talk on the phone before I dipped on him."

"Alright, tell me again from the beginning what happened."

Fanny revisited everything that transpired between Sess and her, not leaving out any details. Diego was formulating a plan in his head.

"What's up with all them bags you just dumped in the back seat?"

"Oh, that's my outfit, shoes and wig for the opening of the new club *Red Bottomz*. Some chick named Tata is opening up a club and she got all the top line entertainment performing—Shy Glizzy, porn star Layla Red and some other chick named Trini will be there. The whole city is coming out for the opening. You probably haven't heard since you been down NC in them woods. When Fanny mentioned the name *Tata*, his ears started ringing. This can't be the same Tata.

"Damn! I know a chick named Tata—I wonder if this the same Tata," Diego stated.

Fanny booted up her IG account. She did a little scrolling through her phone until she found what she was looking for "Is this her?" Fanny asked, holding the phone so Diego could see. "This Tata has been doing a lot of advertisement on IG about the club opening," Fanny stated. Diego couldn't believe his eyes as he saw Tata standing sexy in front of a beautiful Porsche truck.

Jibril Williams

Chapter 20

The next night

"I would feel much better if you were going out to the club with me tonight," Fanny said with a sad face, trying to put on her best act. She was hoping that he would continue to decline her request. She didn't believe in taking sand to the beach, so there was no need on taking Diego to the club with her when she had the intention of going to the club to bag a nigga with that check, but in case she didn't come up tonight, she could come back to the hotel and bounce on Diego's fat ole dick for the night.

"Naw, I'm good. I got some shit to handle but when you done I'll be at the room waiting on you."

"Okay!" Fanny said, quickly stepping out Diego's car. The way that her white Versace dress was hugging her hips and showing off the bottom of her chocolate butt cheeks when she stepped out Diego's car, made him want to tell her to jump in the backseat real quick so he could jump dead in her pussy for a quickie. But he had major shit to do, so he pushed the thought to the back of his mind. Fanny got into her Kia, and Diego murked out. Twenty minutes later, he was sitting in Columbia Heights Village Apartments' complex on Columbia Rd NW.

He could see Sess's white Tahoe parked in front of his building.

Diego turned down the Meek Mills he was listening to, and racked a bullet in the chamber of his .45. He picked up his phone and called Sess.

"Where you at, Slim?" Sess stated the instant he answered the phone, recognizing Diego's number.

"Meet me on Benning Road at the gas station. The one before you cross the bridge.

"Aye, Slim, what you driving? The Lex or something low key?" Diego looked at the phone crazy when he heard Sess's questions.

"I'm in the Lex—Twenty minutes, be there." Diego hung up the phone and made his way to Sess's apartment door. Diego walked quickly with his head down. The hood he wore concealed his face. He could feel the sweat starting to trickle down his back under his hoodie. Sess lived on the first floor, which was ground level. His apartment was the first one on the left as soon as you entered the building. Diego stood in front of apartment #1 with the .45 at his side. He could hear Sess talking through the door.

"He's gonna meet me on Benning Road in twenty minutes, just make sure you bring—" Sess paused his conversation, as he opened his apartment door and saw Diego on the other side of his door. Diego pointed his burner at him and held a finger to his lips, subjecting Sess to be quiet. Diego took the phone from Sess and listened to the person Sess had been talking to: "Don't worry about the money, Mr. Hines just make sure Diego Ross is there. I'm calling in the tactical takedown team. I will be in touch." The phone went dead.

"Damn, Sess, you was gonna sell a nigga out to twelve," Diego said, backing Sess up into his apartment, kicking the door close with his foot.

"Man, what you talking about?" Sess said, trying to play Diego for stupid, as he backed up into the middle of the living room.

"You was gonna sell me out for a punk ass thirty bands, Slim! Slim! Me, Slim? My people help feed you, but you know what? Fanny told me that you the worse type of fuck nigga."

Sess placed a confused look on his face and Diego caught the look.

"If it wasn't for Fanny bringing to my attention that you was a grimy nigga that can't be trusted, you would be thirty bands richer. While I was pounding her guts out, all I could do was think about killing you, but first I had to see if she had any truth to her words and hearing your bitch ass through the door talking with twelve is all the proof I need." Diego gripped his .45 "On your knees, nigga!" Diego ordered.

Sess looked like he wanted to make a break for, it but there was nowhere to go but head-on into the bullets Diego had for him if he made the wrong move. He reluctantly dropped to his knees. Tears of fear started to roll down his cheeks.

"Diego, shit ain't what you think it is, bruh. A nigga fuck up out here in these streets. The PCP got my mind cloudy, bruh. Come on, D, spare a nigga." Sess's plea fell on deaf ears. Diego hated rats. He hated a muthfucka who used the law to settle their beef or use the law as a means to come up by cashing a nigga in for reward money. Diego walked towards Sess, flipped the burner over in his hand where he was gripping the barrel. He brought the handle down on Sess's temple, knocking him out cold. Diego then took the opportunity to snatch the lamp cords from both lamps that were stationed at the end of the "L" shape sofa. He tucked the burner in the small of his back, and draped the cords around his neck. He grabbed Sess by his ankles and dragged him to the apartment's small bathroom. He tied Sess's hands and feet together behind his back. Sess looked like a human scorpion. Sweat started to build up on Diego's forehead. He lifted Sess's body over the lip of the tub. He felt pain in his abdominal area where his colostomy bag was located. He had to sit on the edge of the tub to get his bearings. The pain in his stomach had him feeling slightly woozy. Diego took a few deep breaths and regained his composure. He hoped by him straining, he didn't damage something in his abdominal or—worse—damage his intestines. Looking down at Sess's punk ass, Diego became mad. "Fuck nigga was gonna turn me in for reward money." Sess's head was leaking from the gash Diego gave him when he hit him with his gun. "Wake ya bitch ass up!" *Whoop!* Diego gave Sess a backhand slap in the back of his head.

Sess started to stir. Diego gave him another slap. *Whoop!* Sess came through; he struggled against the lamp cords that bounded him. He lay on his stomach with his feet and hands tied together behind his back. Blood from the gash started to run into Sess's left eye, making it difficult for him to see with it.

"Aye, Diego, you don't have to do this shit, Slim—No harm came to you," Sess said through tears. Diego took a wash cloth off the towel rack and shoved it in Sess's mouth. He then stuffed another towel in the drain of the tub. Diego turned both hot and cold on the tub, and water immediately began to rush in the tub, slowly filling the tub up. Diego lowered the toilet lid and took a seat. He fished a crumbled pack of Newports from his pocket, and removed a smoke from the pack. He lit one with a match.

Sess was trying to speak through the wash cloth in his mouth, but it was futile. Diego took a pull of the cigarette, and blew a cloud of smoke in the bathroom air. "You know, Slim, they say drowning is the worst possible death known to man," Diego stated, not looking at Sess but at the cloud of smoke that slowly danced in the air from the cigarette. Sess thrashed in the tub. It seemed like the more he fought, the tighter the cords became around his ankles and wrist.

The water in the tub was above Sess's chin. He had to arch his neck to keep the water from rushing into his mouth and nose. Diego took another pull of the cancer stick. Sess screamed through the gag in his mouth.

"I—aaaaaaah!" He continued to fight. His neck started to get tired and crampy. Sess lowered his chin into the tub's water; water rushed in his mouth and nose. He arched his neck again trying to keep the water out.

"You know, Sess, when it's your time to go, you just have to embrace the moment. Fanny is not coming, she's out at that new club called Red Bottomz, trying to come up in a nigga check. Later on tonight I'm gonna be fucking the dog shit outta her and you won't even be on her mind. Inhale the water, Sess, so I can go get lost in Fanny good hot wet pussy. Inhale the water so you won't have to feel the pain of life anymore, inhale, nigga!" Diego screamed. By this time, the water was up past Sess's nose. No matter how far he arched his neck back, he couldn't stop the water from entering his body. Sess went into his last line of defense. He held his breath, but with all the smoking he had in his life, his lungs weren't equipped to hold his breath long. His lungs gave, and water rushed in. Sess's body twitched and jerked hard. Diego sat there and watched. Sess lay still in the tub water. Brownish liquid started to seep from the back of Sess's jeans. Diego could smell the stench from Sess's bowels breaking. He turned the tub water off and killed the bathroom lights, as he closed the door behind him. He had club Red Bottomz on his mind.

Jibril Williams

Chapter 21

Red Bottom Squad turned the fuck up! Phatmama shouted as she threw a fistful of Franklins on top of the stripper that was having a twerk-off contest in front of her and Boot. The bills rained down on the strippers. Some of the bills stuck to the women's bodies from the coat of sweat they had worked up from making their ass cheek clap so hard. Boot had the money gun, and was shooting bills in between the cheeks of a light-skinned stripper from out of Houston Texas named Fendi Blue. It seemed like every bill that Boot shot from his money gun, the stripper was catching it with her cheeks like they were hands. Boot was acting a fool too. He was slapping Fendi Blue's cheeks, adding extra waves to her already jiggling cheeks. Phatmama wasn't even fazed by Boot's actions. She'd already given him the green light to indulge himself as long they wallowed in the indulgence together. How she viewed it was, if Boot and her was good enough to kill niggas together, then they damn sure could fuck hoes together. What was done in the light wasn't a mystery to her.

Whip, Billie, Racks and members of D.C.B. played the other side of the VIP section. They were being entertained by eight strippers. The strippers all worked their lovely luscious tatted bodies to Jhene Aiko and H.E.R. track B.S. The VIP was packed; money was flipping through the air. Whip wasn't turning up like his men were, especially Boot, but he tossed a few bills over the women. He played the background and watched his team wild out. He had stopped Pound from getting his manhood waxed in the corner of the VIP in front of the whole team. If it wasn't for this being Tata's establishment, he wouldn't have gave a fuck, but he broke that shit up quick and told Pound to take that shit to one of the private rooms. Pound didn't want to leave all the excitement for some wet neck, so he tipped the click eater $100 and got back to partying. Whip watched his team and was proud of what he had put together. He knew that it was so much more he wanted to do than sell dope and gang bang. Every member of D.C.B. wore a chain of the nation's capital with D.C.B. going through it in red diamonds. Whip took a pull of the burning Vega that he held in his hand, and chased the take with a swig from his black bottle. Whip's black Nationals cap with the red "W" sat low over his eyes. The all-black billionaire jeans and shorts were crispy fresh, along with his all-red air maxs. Whip was a hood nigga to the core, but he had corporate world dreams. The strip club was in full swing. Whip looked out from the VIP section, and admired Tata's success. Drinks were being poured, bottles were being ordered, and money was being distributed to the entertainers as if it was toilet paper by the rolls. Players from the Washington Wizards and the Nationals—baseball teams—had the club going crazy. Every nigga in the club was trying to outdo them. Whip shook his head. Didn't these street niggas know that the athletes' money was much longer than theirs! There was no way that the hustlers' money could compare, unless you were El Chapo or somebody. Tata came in the VIP section, looking sexier than Whip had ever seen her. The peach Fendi dress was body-gripping. Whip had to bite down on his lip, seeing her. Tata had her hair braided in two cornrows: one on each side of her head. The extended eyelashes she wore had her looking like a chocolate covered baby doll. She was murdering them with the Fendi print on her nails that matched the black Fendi Red Bottom she wore.

"Papi, I knew you ain't up here faking like you ain't enjoying yourself—Look at all this booty in here," Tata stated, kissing Whip on the cheek.

"I'm good, woman, and I'm enjoying myself."

"Well, why you holding the VIP wall up? You suppose to be bussing up on these bitches, Papi."

Whip chuckled. "A boss don't always have to show that he is a boss—Real bosses move in silence, baby," Whip replied, running his thumb over Tata's juicy lips. Tata didn't reply verbally, but she turned her back to Whip and started slow grinding her backside on him. Whip's love stick grew in his jeans. Tata's softness instantly aroused him. Whip pushed his pelvis into Tata's prominent booty. Whip ran his hand up Tata's thick thighs. The softness of her skin had Whip wanting to fuck her right there. He was fighting not to go up Tata's dress and cuff her phat pussy.

Even though the crew was being entertained by the strippers, Whip knew that there was at least a pair of eyes on him at all times. That was how the game was; someone was always watching. He didn't want members of his team to see him handle Tata in such a way that they may directly or indirectly disrespect her somewhere in the near future.

Tata ground harder into Whip's lap. The way Whip touched her always put heat to that hot pocket between her legs. Whip's rod fought to be freed from his jeans. His dick was harder than a pogo stick. For a while, Tata was cautious about who knew that Whip and her were feeling each other. However, as time went on, and Tata had grown even closer to Whip, Tata was in love with the bifocal-wearing gangsta "Bae, you keep working your ass like that up against this wood—I'm gonna have to take you to your office and break in that new desk you got in there," Whip stated in Tata's ear. Tata turned around with an amazing smile on her face, and a lustful fire in her eyes that said, *Try me!* Whip grabbed Tata by the hand, and started leading the way to her office, but her vibrating phone in her hand stopped her. "Damn!" she mumbled after reading the text. "Baby, the main event is about to start—We got to go down to the main stage, we gonna have to break that desk in later," Tata spoke in Whip's ear over the club music.

"Let's get this bag, boss lady," Whip stated, letting Tata know he understood. He informed his team that he was moving, and they fell in line behind him and Tata

Tata made it down on the club floor where the DJ handed her a wireless mic, and she went into straight boss mode. "What it do, y'all!" she addressed the club; the music stopped. "Is everyone having a good time?" Tata asked, and the club roared with cheers. "I appreciate everyone that came out tonight to support Red Bottomz grand opening and showing a diva mad love." The club broke out into cheers, and the hustlers and money getters held up some type of bottle in the air, showing Tata much respect. "I got something special tonight for you all. I bring you pornstar Trini Calypso and Layla Red. The curtains on the round stage lifted, and Cardi B's track—*Thru Your Phone*—came through the speakers. Layla Red lay on her back with Trini on top of her in the sixty-nine position. The club went into a frenzy. All types of niggas rushed the stage with bricks of money in their hands. Trini was sucking and nibbling on Layla Red's clit and pussy to the rhythm of Cardi B's track. Layla Red had Trini's ass cheeks spread far apart; she had Trini's whole pussy in her mouth. She was locked on Trini's pussy like it was her last supper. The club occupants were throwing so much money on the stage that it looked like it was a money storm right over top of the sexy women.

Two more strippers walked on stage and stood over the porn stars, as they feasted on each other. They shook up bottles of Ace of Spades and shot the bubbly on top Trini and Layla Red, like two men would do if they were shooting their load on the women. The scene looked so sexy and exotic. Tata wasn't into the girl-on-girl thing, but watching the two women made her feel a certain way because a gush of wetness saturated her pantie line.

Whip backed out the crowd that was around the stage. Tata followed him. She was wondering what the matter with Whip was. Whip made his way over to where Sticks was standing on the couch in one of the booths. He was looking over the crowd and enjoying the view from a distance. "What's the fuck up with you niggas? All the action is around the stage," Tata said.

Whip and Sticks started laughing. Whip addressed Tata: "Bae, we good right here. With all that ass and pussy on stage, there's nothing but hard dicks around that stage, and it's too packed up there to bullshit around and take a chance of bumping into a nigga rod. I'm good, bae."

"I'm good back here, boss lady," Sticks said, turning a black bottle up to his lips.

Tata burst out laughing. A barmaid walked over and whispered something in Tata's ear. "Shit!" Tata mouthed. "Okay, get word to the women that they need to cash their cards in for cash soon as possible," Tata instructed the barmaid. Cindy was one of Rau'f's workers. He lent Tata his club staff so she could have business run smoothly without a hiccup. Tata was grateful to Rau'f.

"Is everything alright?" Whip asked.

"Yeah, everything's cool. Cindy just informed me that we have sold out the private room cards."

"Shit, business booming!" Whip said happily, kissing Tata on the cheek.

"What's up, blood!" a tall stocky nigga said, walking to Sticks, throwing a blood sign with his right hand. Whip instantly didn't like the dude. He looked kinda square, and the look on Whip's face showed that he didn't like the dude

"What's good, Kirby?" Sticks said, but not acknowledging the gang sign that Kirby displayed.

"Aye, Sticks, who's the clown?" Whip asked.

Kirby was slightly offended by Whip's comment. The two men shared stares.

"This here is my buzzin—My mother's oldest sister's son."

"Make him disappear, his vibe isn't right with me," Whip stated, still eye-wrestling with Kirby. Sticks leaned over and whispered in Whip's ear.

"Listen, blood, I was thinking about putting this nigga on pay roll. He works over D.C. jail. We got a few homies over there we can touch and also if one turn rat in our organization we could easy find out. My buzzin has always been down for the cause. He's not blood yet. He's a sympathizer."

Whip understood clearly why Sticks wanted to bring Kirby on board, but Whip had a thing about turning thirty-something-year-old men to gang members. If you're thirty-something, trying to be a gang banger, something's wrong, but he could not turn the opportunity down. Whip dug in his pocket and pulled off three bands from his knot.

"You deal with Sticks—and Sticks only—enjoy yourself tonight on me," Whip said, handing Kirby the money. Kirby looked at Sticks, and nodded before he walked off. Whip watched Kirby's back.

"Aye, Sticks, you responsible for him. Make that shit work."

"Ain't no question," Sticks said, turning up the bottle to his lips.

Jibril Williams

Chapter 22

"This muthafucka look live as fuck! Jelli said, stepping outta her new G wagon that came with a hefty price tag which she paid for with cash straight off the lot. She had treated herself to feeling the need to enjoy the fruits of her labor. Jelli heard from Zodio about the Red Bottomz grand opening even though she had written off wearing Red Bottoms, because it was a Red Bottom Squad thing, and she wasn't rockin' with them bitches no more on any level. But tonight she made an exception to the rule. It was broadcast for weeks now. If you showed up to the event without a pair of Red Bottoms on your feet, you would be turned away. Jelli refused to be denied access to the club because she came to turn up and show out. The black and white Fendi printed pants she wore accentuated her curves. The pants fitted Jelli like a glove. Jelli's black and white Fendi shirt complemented the Red Bottoms she wore. She grabbed her oversized Fendi bag off the floor of the truck, while Fate made his way around to the passenger side to escort Jelli inside the club. Jelli invited her whole distributing team out. Everyone came out with at least two shooters and a bag full of money. Merely looking at this fucking parking lot, you can tell that it's money in the club, especially by the cars that were sitting out here in the parking lot. "I swear I saw like two Buggattis out this bitch," Sparko said, pulling up and hopping out of his Mercedes Benz 600 Coupé.

"Man, I'm ready to see what this spot got to offer—I done heard so much shit about this place on the radio and on IG. I'm ready to see if it's all talk or it's the real deal," Fatts said, running a hand over his goatee.

"Oh this definitely the spot to be let go, gents," Jelli said, walking towards the club. Flame wasn't too thrilled about being out with his connect tonight, and he didn't like how she had everyone surrounded around her like she was the last don or some shit. He believed that the strip club was too flashy for his taste, yet he believed in keeping strong business ties. He trailed behind her with his shooters.

My fuckin' man, Fate! What it do, Slim?" the club head security said, as Fate walked.

"Ain't too much, just moving like a crook moves under the radar," Fate replied, giving the bouncer some dap.

"Shit, impossible to be under the radar coming to an establishment like this on a night that every name with some clout and every hitta is in the building."

"Boss lady wants to relax and enjoy herself tonight, so it is what it is and here's a token to make shit happen." Fate palmed the bouncer a stack of bills.

The bouncer knew that the payment was to let Fate and his people in without being searched. He waved them in like it was his club. "Enjoy yourself, Fate."

"I plan to," Fate replied.

Once Jelli and her people made it in, the crowd was dispensing from around the main stage. Two buck naked chicks had pushed brooms, pushing and sweeping money from off stage into two big black trash bags. Jelli and her team found a booth at the far left corner and posted up. Jelli waved a waitress over. "Let me get twenty bottles of Ace of Spades and five bottles of Patron." The waitress's eyes bucked.

"Okay, coming right up," the skinny caramel-complexioned waitress stated.

"And send ten of your prettiest and sexiest strippers, and let them know that a real live diva is in the building," Jelli said, sitting her Fendi bag beside her.

"Ain't no muthafuckin question about that!" Sparko yelled, looking at all the sexy women running and strutting through the club. The scene looked like a lap dance city. It was like every nigga in there was getting a lap dance, or bitches were having private twerk-offs in front of groups of niggas while they popped bottles over them and threw money in the air.

"This shit live as fuck! I appreciate you inviting us out Sparko stated, pulling out a zip of some diesel bug, then he started twisting up. The waitress came back with the ordered drinks, along with a train of bad bitches, and the woman didn't waste time helping them turn up. Jelli sat on the edge of her seat with her legs wide open, sitting like she was a dude, with a burning Vega hanging from the corner of her mouth. She lustfully watched the woman in front of her work her body to the music of Kevin Gates' *Love Bug*. Jelli seductively threw bills on the stripper. The stripper went into a full split, then rolled to her back and stretched her legs wide open in front of Jelli. The stripper pushed the material of her thong to the side, and dipped two fingers into her wet box.

Jelli and the sexy babe held an intense stare. Jelli bit down on her bottom lip. When Jelli was doing time in the pen, she was introduced to the pillow princess life—That something that women indulge in while they are on lock. That's when they let a secret admirer eat them out. But at the same time, claim they are only bi-sexual because they all on lock. Jelli hadn't been touched since Cain died, and her hormones were going haywire. She could feel the slushiness between the lips of her creases. Soon the crotch of her

Fendi pants will be soaking wet, due to her not completing her outfit with a pair of panties. Jelli wondered, *Could ol' girl eat a pussy?*

***

"I know that everyone is to get back to the action down stairs, but I had Tata and Whip call this meeting in the office tonight because this is the only time I had the opportunity to get D.C.B. and the Red Bottom Squad in one place at one time." Boot was nervous as hell; his forehead was coated with a light sheen of sweat. He took a pull of the overstuffed Backwood and passed it to Racks.

All eyes were on Boot. Sticks stood to the side with his arm swapped over Billie. Whip reached over and grabbed Tata's hand. "There comes a time in life where a king finds his queen, a pimp finds his bottom bitch, a con finds his gooniest." Boot swallowed the spit that was formulating in his mouth before he continued talking. "It's my time," Boot said, throwing up his b's. I found my queen, I found my bottom bitch, I found my gangstress. All is left to do is ask, would she live for me and spend the rest of her life with me? Boot took a knee in front of Phatmama and displayed a red Tiffany's box with the red princess cut diamond resting on a black titanic band. Boot looked up at Phatmama; her eye misted over as she held her manicured hands over her mouth.

"Ms. Tanya Phatmama Foxy, would you be my wifey?" Boot asked. Now it was Phatmama's time to swallow the excess spit in her mouth. Tata squeezed Whip's hand with excitement. The room was silent, waiting on Phatmama's response to Boot's proposal. All you could hear was the muffles from the club speakers.

"Boot!" Phatmama cleared her throat. I can be your queen, I can be your gangstress, but I can't be your bottom bitch. The only way that I could be your wife, I have to be your only bitch!"

"I won't have it any other way," Boot said, standing, placing the 2 ½ karat on his woman's finger. Phatmama tongued Boot, telling him she loved him through their kisses. The room exploded in cheers and *soo-woos*.

"Let's make a toast!" Tata yelled, pouring drinks for everyone. Everyone held a drink in their hands. "A toast to love, money, success, and many blessings to come, to Boot and Phatmama!" Tata announced, as she and the group downed their shots of Patron.

"D.C.B. first lady, y'all!" Boot said, wrapping his arm around Phatmama."

"Let me look at that ring, Phatmama," Tata stated, step-ping over to Phatmama and Boot. "Damn, this bitch is pretty—I never seen an engagement ring like this—This shit different but it's sexy," Tata said, holding Phatmama's hand in her hand. "What's the meaning behind it?" Tata asked. Phatmama looked at Boot.

"The black titanic band represents me—strong and black. The red diamond represents Phatmama—sexy, beau-tiful and precious. She's the centerpiece that brings light to my dark world." Boot's statement fucked Tata up mentally. She wasn't expecting something that deep from Boot. "I wish you all the best. May you have—" Tata's sentence was cut short, as her attention was drawn to the club security monitors. She watched Jelli and her people turn up and throw money in the air over a crowd of strippers. Jelli wasn't what made Tata sick to her stomach. It was the fact that Jelli was wearing the princess crown that Zoey was sup-posed to buried with—the very crown that held the two black diamonds.

Chapter 23

"Damn, the whole city out this bitch!" Diego mumbled to himself. He crept through the parking lot of Red Bottomz. He circled the parking lot a second time he'd seen a whip that looked very familiar to him. He stopped the Chrysler 300 in front of the silver Mercedes Benz 600 Coupé. He peeped the tag on the whip. Just like he thought, the car belonged to Sparko. He pulled off and found a parking spot that enabled him to see the front door of the club and Sparko's Benz. Diego settled in and sparked a pre-rolled Backwood. He felt like tonight was going to be a long night.

***

"I got to piss badder than a muthafucker," Flame said, getting up from the booth. His two shooters followed behind him.

"You want me to go with you, handsome? I can hold it for you?" the sexy stripper named Apple asked. She'd been dancing and exposing all her goodies to Flame and his men.

"No, baby, I can manage just fine, but I'll be back and we can talk about some arrangement for later," Flame said over his shoulder

Tata's nostrils flexed with anger as she made her way over towards Jelli and her team. The Red Bottom Squad and D.C.B. was right on her heels.

"We fuckin' this bitch up tonight, Tata!" Phatmama said.

Tata said nothing. She just kept pushing through the club. Fate saw Tata and Phatmama making their way over toward them with a bunch of niggas who he assumed was Tata's hittas. He tapped Jelli on the leg and nodded towards the approaching group.

Jelli wasted no time. She stood up and drew her weapon and let it rest against her leg, and the men around her did the same. The D.C.B. crew carried all types of hammers. Tata walked into Jelli's face and pressed her gun into her stomach. Jelli placed her gun into Tata's rib.

"Bitch, you brought your stank ass in my club, you're not welcome here!" Tata said through clenched teeth.

"Damn, this how you embrace a bitch after you kill her man!—her husband?" Jelli retorted with a sinister smile on her face.

"Fuck you and that nigga Cain!"

"Naw, baby girl, fuck you and Zoey!" Jelli shot back. Hearing Zoey's name was like a hot knife being pushed through Tata's heart. Tata's eyes went to the crown that rested on Jelli's head.

"You got something that belongs to us?" Tata said, nodding toward the crown.

"Bitch, please! I don't have shit that belongs to you. This shit was a debt that you failed to pay me. I had to get my cut from the black diamonds. What? You thought I forgot?"

Tata added some pressure on her trigger. "Bitch, give me the crown before I put three holes in your head like a bowling ball."

"Yeah, right, hoe! What you gonna do? Shoot me in front of all the people? If you do that, you would have to plead out to a life sentence. Bitch, I'm not gonna give you shit but a bullet to your face when I catch you in them street." Jelli spoke with venom.

Tata wanted to air Jelli ass out right there in the middle of the club, but Jelli was right. There were too many people in the club, and the club occupants already started to peep what was transpiring between them. Muthafuckas already had their phones out, recording the scene. "In the streets is where we will cook this beef, make sure you keep them lighters on you," Tata said, turning in her heels.

Jelli lingered on the back of Tata's head before she gathered her belongings and exited the club, vowing to kill Tata.

"Naw, fuck that! We just letting this bitch leave without no gun play!" Racks complained but her complaint fell on deaf ears, as everyone made their way back toward the club office. "Aye, Taz, I need you' to ride out with me," said Racks.

"What!" Blood, it's gonna be a time and place for all that. Besides, Whip or Boot didn't give us the green light to do anything."

Taz found some music on the radio, as he kept his eyes glued to the tail lights of the truck. "Racks, I don't like this spirit of the moment shit."

"Damn, nigga, what the fuck!—I got to check our G card or something—We haven't been rolling ten minutes yet and we bitching," Rack said in frustration.

"Taz looked at Rack like she was crazy. He put it in his mental to pound her pussy out when this shit was all said and done.

Jelli and Fate hit Suitland Parkway. The traffic was thin, so it wasn't hard keeping up with the truck. Racks sat on the passenger side with the TEC-9 on her lap, and her heart racing. Her mind was consumed with thoughts of Zoey. She missed the hell out of her. Her eyes misted over, thinking about her friend. Racks pulled her hat low over her eyes to avoid Taz seeing her cry "This for Zoey," Rack mumbled.

"So how you want to do this, blood?" Taz broke Racks' thoughts with his question.

"I really don't know. I prefer we catch them at a light and let me empty the whole clip on their asses."

"Fuck, man! Is you fucking crazy? They got traffic cameras everywhere in the parkway. We might have followed them all the way to their crib."

***

"Ahhh, fuck!" Diego said, relieving his bladder in between the cars where he was parked at. He shook his wood, put it back into his jeans, and climbed back into the Chrysler 300. He went to roll a Backwood, but the sight of Jelli and Fate coming out of club Red Bottomz—along with the family elite distributors—had him feeling a certain way. He didn't know what the fuck they were up to, but he wasn't feeling the fact that they were out partying while he was out on the lamb ducking and dodging 'twelve' for a murder he didn't commit. He had to push them thought to the side when he saw Tata's people rush out the club and started tailing Jelli and Fate. He tried to start the car, but all he got was a clicking sound when he turned the key in the ignition. "Come on, bitch, start!" Diego yelled, trying to start the car again. He grabbed his phone and tried to call Fate. The phone went straight to voicemail. He tried the number again and got the same result. "Fuck it!" Diego said, sending Fate a voice message, letting him know the opposition was trailing him. However, before he could send the message, his driver side window exploded.

Chapter 24

Tata's elbows rested on her office desk. She had her hands stippled in front of her, trying to calm her nerves. She was stark raving mad.

She couldn't believe Jelli had a clit big enough to show face in the club, wearing the princess crown that was meant to be buried with Zoey. It was bad enough the bitch was posting pics of the crown on the Gram, but to show up in person wearing it took shit to a whole different level. Tata didn't want to just shoot Jelli, but she wanted to gut her like a pig, hang her upside down, and split her down the middle, and let her insides fall out. Billie pulled Tata a straight shot of Patron and placed it in front of her.

"What's going through your mind, mami?" Phatmama asked, sparking a Backwood.

"Murder!" Tata replied, picking the shot of Patron up and downing it, and handing the glass back to Billie for a refill.

"Shit, I'm about that life, let's bust a move," Phatmama took a heavy pull of the Backwood.

"We need to supply some pressure on Jelli, we need to shake shit up—The bitch has gotten way too comfortable," Billie said, pouring her own shot of Patron.

"Naw, let's stop house playing with this bitch and go straight at this bitch guns blazing and smash this bitch like a fuckin' rodent she is, and be done with her." Phatmama spoke up, blowing smoke in the air.

"We need more intel on the bitch, we must make sure she—"

Tata was cut off by the knock at the door. Whip walked in.

"Everything good in here?" Whip asked, as he glanced over the room.

"We good in here but have you found Racks yet?" Tata retorted.

"I don't know where Racks is, but I think we just hit pay dirt with this Jelli business." Hearing this news made everyone in the room stand up.

"What is it?" Tata asked anxiously. Whip's phone rang; he saw it was Boot, so he answered it.

"What's up, blood?"

Tata and them couldn't hear the convo from the other side of the phone, but all they could hear was Whip telling whoever to sit on the nigga until him and Tata could make it over there. Whip disconnected the call and went to open the office door. A slim dude stopped in the office, rocking a low fade. "I want you to meet Flame.

***

"These bitches been riding for a minute—It's not like they going to a specific destination, they just riding, Racks—You think they figured out we tailing them?" Taz asked, checking his rear and side mirrors.

"Naw, I don't think they on to us, blood, they just riding," Racks said, climbing into the back seat. "We gonna catch the red light that's coming up, pull up on the passenger side; this bitch about to catch the hold clip," Racks mouthed, tying the towel around her face. The light caught red. Taz checked his mirrors one last time before pulling beside Jelli's G wagon. He didn't see anything behind them but a black Ram 1500 truck easing beside Jelli and Fate. He lined the Altima up next to Jelli's passenger door; he could slightly see Jelli through the truck tints. Racks let the window down and stuck the TEC-9 out the window, and rode the trigger. The gun erupted in the night. Bullet after bullet hit Jelli's truck but nothing happened. Bullets after bullets bounced off the truck. Jelli just sat there looking at Racks, smiling and smoking a blunt. A bullet ricocheted off the truck door and hit Taz in the head, causing this fool to slip from the brakes of the Altima, and causing the car to drift into traffic. The Ram truck reared the Altima hard, making Racks drop the TEC-9 in the streets. "Drive this bitch, blood!" Racks yelled. The traffic was light and—thanks to Taz drifting—the car wasn't hit by oncoming traffic, as it coasted into oncoming traffic. Racks saw Taz's head tilted. This was the first time she saw the blood and hole in his head. The car coasted through traffic without getting hit. By this time, the light had turned green and Jelli's wagon made a left, but the Ram truck flooded it and rammed Taz's Altima. The impact caused the car to crash, and Racks to blackout.

***

Flame took a drag of his Newport. "Why give us the info about Jelli?" Tata asked. You could tell Flame was a real street nigga, but you could tell that he was the sophisticated and smart type. Flame let out a cloud of smoke.

"I hold no loyalty to Jelli when it comes to her going to war with any branch of bloods," Flame spoke, taking another pull of the Newport.

"But nothing is free so what do you want for this info?" Tata asked.

"You are right, nothing is free, but I figure one hand washes the other type of deal."

"Meaning?" Tata asked.

Once you hit Jelli, I'm sure I'm going to need a new plug. I hear that D.C.B.'s got access to some grade A dope. I would like to purchase product from y'all."

"I just don't see you selling Jelli out just for a connect— You could just side with Jelli and still have a plug—It's something more to it, Flame," Whip said.

"And there is Cain. Well, as Jelli had made a great mistake by allowing their distributors to know who everyone was, I have this knowledge. If Jelli is eliminated, I would like for you to supply me and I will supply Jelli distribution team."

"So by you becoming their supplier, your slice of the pie becomes greater. But who says after this you won't go out and shop for another supplier or try to connect directly with a plug?"

"If we made a deal on blood, then that's what it is," Flame stated firmly. Whip could see that Flame was serious. Even though he was the plug that Flame would be dealing with if the deal went through, it was Tata's call. He looked at his queen for an answer. Tata slightly nodded. Whip shook Flame's hand. "We have a deal, blood, but if you fuck over me, I will spill yours all over this city," Whip spoke in a whisper.

"Flame made eye contact with Whip. "Don't need to stress that to me, but know that goes both ways. So what's understood doesn't need to be spoken. We finna made millions, blood. Jelli had twenty major distributors around this Maryland and VA line getting ready to eat on a real *boss* level." Flame shook Whip's hand again and walked out the office.

"Shit, that was intense," Tata said.

"I know, right! I hope we can trust him," Phatmama said.

"It's not over yet—Boot caught Diego outside the club—They got him held at a spot waiting on us," Whip said.

"Shit! Well, let's go," Tata said.

"Naw," Whip said, kissing Tata on the forehead. "You and Billie stay and watch over the club. The D.C.B.'s are still here on standby. Me and Phatmama is going to head over to the house and see what we gon' get at this nigga Diego."

"Keep me informed," Tata said, watching Whip walk out her office.

Jibril Williams

Chapter 25

"Fuck you! Fuck you bitch ass nigga, kill me!" Diego fought the words through his swollen jaw. His left eye was shut completely; this was the result of Boot repeatedly hitting him with a cross right hook. Diego's left eye held a crimson looking blood clot in it. You could see no white on the eyeball. Two of his teeth laid at his foot; Boot had knocked them out over twenty minutes ago, and his mouth and split lips hadn't stopped bleeding yet. Every time Boot would hit him, the red-nose pitbull would go off, threatening to attack Diego, but wouldn't come out its corner unless Boot commanded the animal to.

"Nigga, all I'm asking you for is a location, that's all." Boot stood over Diego in a pair of black jeans and wife beater that was covered in Diego's blood. When Jelli showed her face in the club, Whip had sent a team of hittas out to hold down the parking lot of club Red Bottomz in case Jelli had a trick up her sleeve. This had paid off when Pound had spotted someone pissing in the parking lot between some cars and then getting back in his whip and continued to watch the front entrance of the club. Pound knew right then this nigga was on some bullshit, and went to snatch his ass up. The spy in question had been none other than Diego. Sweat dripped from Diego's face; every time the sweat would enter the cut under his eye, it would burn like hell. Diego struggled to breathe. He already made up his mind that he was going to die, so giving up information about Jelli or anyone associated with Cain crime family wasn't going to spare his life.

"Jelli location," Diego whispered. Boot held his ear close to Diego's mouth. "Jelli's in hell—Go get her, bitch nigga!" Diego yelled, biting down on Boot's ear, snipping it.

"Agghh, bitch! Rose, hit!" Boot shouted at the pitbull in the corner. The dog came out the corner like a bullet, hurling at Diego, hitting him in the midsection, knocking the chair he was sitting in over. Diego yelled as Rose's canines sunk down into his stomach, aggravating his whole stomach wound from being shot in the stomach. The colostomy bag ripped open, defiling the basement air. Rose shook her big head from left to right. All Diego could do was, scream and hope that Boot would kill him soon and quickly. His arms were tied behind his back, and his feet were duct-taped to the legs of the chair. Members of D.C.B. looked on with no remorse in their eyes. Most of their heads bobbed up and down to the track of Shy Glizzy that came from the basement speakers. "Break!" Boot yelled, and Rose released Diego from her jaws and trotted back to her corner, where she waited for her master's next command. Boot brought his hand away from his ear, and it was smeared with his blood. Boot stomped Diego in the chest several times before he sat the chair Diego was strapped to back upright. Just then, Whip came down the basement stairs with Phatmama. Whip stopped in front of Diego. He looked at the battered prisoner and smiled. Diego could feel a presence in front of him. He looked up and stared at Whip with his only eye he could see with.

**

The concrete that Racks laid on was cold to her skin. It seemed like every bone and muscle in her body hurt. She couldn't see anything because she was blindfolded. But she could smell the weed burning in the air, and she could also hear the inhale and exhaling of the smoker. They say when one of your senses is taken away from you, it heightens another; at this moment, Racks believed this to be true because her ears and nose had become her eyes. "Untie me!" Racks said, trying her hand to see if she could get a dialog going with whoever it was in the room. No reply came. Racks went on: "I know that you still there because I can smell the weed you smoking. If you not gonna untie, at least let me hit the blunt." Racks did not really think her captor was going to let her smoke, but hearing movement and a hand grabbing the back of her head let her know she was on to something. Racks' hands and feet were chained behind her. "Inhale!" was what Rack heard before he felt a blunt placed to her lips. She inhaled deeply. She could tell the weed was rolled in a cherry flavored Backwood. She and D.C.B.'s often smoked the brand. The weed hit her lungs, and she held it in. The potent weed took over. She could hear the rhythm of her heartbeat. She let out the smoke and took another pull before her captor pulled the Backwood from her lips and released the back of her head. From the voice of the kidnapper and the sweet womanly fragrance the kidnapper wore, Racks could tell that she was in the presence of a woman. She could remember everything that took place that led her here: She and Taz following Jelli and Fate—Taz got shot in the head—The bullets from her TEC-9 not penetrating the Benz wagon door or window. She even remembered being rammed from the back before she blacked out, but she didn't remember how she got where she was. Her thoughts went back to Taz; another member of D.C.B.'s blood was on her hands. First, it was her cousin—Gunz—who died in a botched robbery that she coordinated, and now Taz was gone behind another failed plan she had put together.

"You know much as I hated you, I got to give you some points for trying your hand at killing me." Hearing the voice, Racks knew it was none other than Jelli's.

"I wish I would have succeeded," Racks said.

"Ha! I bet you woulda, but when you a boss bitch like me, you ride around in bullet-proof whips." Jelli chuckled. "Oh, by the way, I been knew y'all was following me. I had some hittas fall back at the club just to make sure Tata didn't send her squad behind us, and she sent your dyke ass!" Jelli's words became harsh. "I always stay a step ahead of you slow ass bitches." Jelli took another pull of her Backwood

"Bitch, fuck you! You gonna get yours in due time."

"Yeah, yeah, I bet I will!" Jelli yelled, putting the blunt out on Racks' face.

"Agghh!" Racks fought to get the burning off of her skin; you could hear Racks' skin sizzle under the heat.

"I'm gonna enjoy torturing you. But I would make it quick if you tell me what I need to know?"

"Bitch, suck my dick!" Racks stated, spitting towards the sound of Jelli's voice.

"Ha-ha! Bitch, you really wish you had one." Jelli started cutting Racks' clothes from her body. Racks' whole body tensed up. "You been running around acting like a nigga, let me see what you got." Cutting Racks' pants and shirt off her body, Jelli broke out into laughter seeing Racks lying there in some polo boxer briefs and her titties held down by ace bandages that she had wrapped around her upper body. "Look at this bitch!—You got your boobies all bounded down like they are a muthafuckin curse or something," Jelli said with her face scrunched up. "Let a bitch see them titties you holding." Jelli cut the ace bandage from Racks' body, and her C-cups fell free. Jelli's eyes ran over

Racks' brown breasts. Racks' areolas were a darker shade of brown. Jelli could tell that Racks' nakedness made her feel funny. Jelli cut the boxer briefs from Racks. "Girl, are you out your mind?" Jelli said. "You need your ass beat for not saving your coochie. You really think you a nigga, huh?" Jelli said, snatching the blindfold off Racks' eyes. It took a few seconds for her eyes to adjust, but once they did, she wished that Jelli would have left it on and just killed her. Standing next to Jelli were two goons who were naked standing over Racks, slow stroking their dicks. Jelli unchained her legs.

"Fuck her, and fuck her good!" Jelli ordered. She sat down on a milk crate and fired up another Backwood. The tallest goon with the fattest wood got down between Racks' legs while the other held Racks' legs apart. Racks tried to fight; it was useless, though. The goon grinned, spitting on Racks' pussy. He took his hand, lubing her opening before forcing his dick into her. He didn't have mercy on Racks. Once he got his length all the way in Racks, he jackhammered into her. Racks' guts were on fire. She'd never had a man inside of her before. She only offered Taz the pussy because she had heard from a few chicks how small he was, but what she was experiencing right now was unbearable. "All you got to do is tell us how to get Tata," Jelli said cheerfully. Racks refused to betray Tata, so she closed her eyes and bit down on her bottom lip in pain.

Jibril Williams

Chapter 26

Three hours later

Diego prayed that Whip would kill him. He didn't know that he could take any more pain that Whip was dishing out. Whip had beaten every inch of Diego's body with a thick rubber mallet. The weapon caused harm to Diego's body, but not enough to break his bones except the bones that were in his fingers. When Whip got tired of beating him, he partook in smoking a blunt with his goons while Rose did the honors of sinking her teeth into his flesh. At that moment, Rose was in him like she was having a treat. Rose had her teeth sunk in his shoulder.

"*Grrrrr grrrr grrrr!*" Rose growled as she shook her head left to right while she ground her teeth into Diego's shoulder.

"Break!" Boot yelled and, just like an obedient servant, Rose trod back to her corner, breathing heavy with her tongue hanging out her head. Rose was one of D.C.B.'s block dogs. She was trained by Boot and Sticks, but pretty much listened to anyone that she was familiar with. "Man, let dead the hoe ass nigga and keep it moving—This nigga ain't talking," Boot said, getting bored at the child's play that Whip was putting down in Diego.

"You ready to start talking, nigga?" Whip said, blazing another Backwood.

Diego cried: "Man, kill me or call my people and get a check for me alive."

"A check! Nigga, how much you think you worth?" Boot asked, amused that the nigga thought he was worth something.

"At least a half a milli," Diego mumbled.

Boot looked at Whip.

"Naw, fuck no! This nigga had something to do with Zoey getting killed." Phatmama upped her Glock 40.

"Hold!" Both Boot and Whip said in sync.

Boot walked next to Phatmama and whispered into her ear. "Phat, I would never go against you on nothing but this situation could lead us to Jelli. If she is willing to pay ransom for this nigga, we could blow the bitch head back on the exchange."

Phatmama was hesitant, but she lowered her gun and took a back seat to the situation. She fished her phone out her back pocket and hit Tata up.

"What's the number, nigga!" Boot mouthed.

Diego coughed up Fate's number. Boot hit him on his burner phone. Boot punched in Fate's number and he answered on the fourth ring.

"Who this?" Fate asked. He normally didn't answer to numbers he didn't recognize.

"It's the muthafuckin boogeyman." A pause came through the line.

"I don't scare and I always been known as a boogieman slayer," Fate clapped back over the phone as he sipped on a shot of Henny.

"I got your boy Diego with me. He thinks he worth a half milli but I think otherwise."

"Fate sat up in his chair, hearing Diego's name. He'd already gotten word that Diego had left the safe house in NC, but he was shocked that he fell in the company of the opposition. "I don't think that is possible, prove it!"

"It would be my pleasure!" Boot took a few pictures of Diego and sent them to Fate. When Fate had gotten the pic, he almost spilled his drink on himself; seeing a battered Diego broke his heart. "Hit me when you get a half a mill bag and ready for me." Boot disconnected the call. Fate jumped out his chair and ran out the room.

***

Racks' womb laid split open; blood and semen leaked from her opening. The soreness between her legs was unbearable. Jelli's goons did their thing on her, working over her pussy and anus, both of which had a heartbeat of their own. It was like when her pussy would throb, her anus would thump, and vice versa. They violated Racks' orifices from every angle. They took turns viciously raping Racks. They even double penetrated her like they were making some sick porn movie. What hurt more than Racks' body was her ego; she never had felt like shit and unworthy as she felt with two different strangers being inside of her. Racks laid on her back. She focused on an oily spot a few feet away from her and tried to let go of the sense of reality that was transpiring around her. She wondered why God was so hard on her. Being a boy trapped in a girl's body was hell. Growing up, she never fit in with the girls she grew up around. The girls were into girly things, and Racks was into things like sports, what latest J's was out. She got along well with the boys. Her only problem was, most of the dudes always tried to fuck her just because they knew she was a female. It was hard to get the dudes to accept her cold heart because she was a female, so she had to go just as hard as the guys she was running with. Racks felt God didn't make shit easy for her. God took her only cousin from her and now he caused her to be where she was butt naked, raped and stripped of her pride and dignity.

"You had enough, lil' nigga?" Jelli asked in a voice of excitement. She watched the entire rape from start to finish. She didn't have a sense of remorse that another woman was being raped right before her eyes. She kicked Racks in her side, making her cough up some blood, and her pussy farted. "Did you have enough?" Jelli asked again but this time her voice held a ton of venom.

Racks took in a deep breath, it was hard for her to breath due to the beating Jelli's goons gave her after they took their turn with her. "Ye—yeah—I—had enough." Racks lifted her head up off the floor. It was hard to see Jelli from the position she was lying in. "Please kill me!" Racks forced the words out her mouth.

"Damn, a little bit of dick got you wanting to die. Damn, girl, you strictly pussy for real." Jelli shook her head in disappointment. "I guess since you ready to die so bad, you are not willing to give up Tata hoe ass." Jelli pulled her smoke-gray Ruger from the small of her back; she squatted down above Racks. She placed the gun to Racks' head. Racks leaned her head against the opening of Jelli's 9mm. Jelli was satisfied with Racks' gesture. It was a sign that Racks had been broken. She was defeated. Jelli's nose wrinkled up; she caught a scent of Racks' bowels. "Oh damn, your shit smell like a nigga for real," Jelli stated, applying some pressure on the gun's trigger.

"Hold up!" Fate said, running into the mechanic area of the auto shop.

"What?" Jelli said in frustration. Fate was out of breath.

"They got Diego!" he announced, holding out the phone toward Jelli.

"Who got Diego? I thought he was in NC somewhere?" Jelli stood to her feet and accepted the phone from him. She saw a horrific pic of Diego's beaten face; you could tell that he was barely hanging on to his life.

"Tata and them got him. We got to get him back, they want a half a mill for him."

Jelli was furious that Tata had gotten one of hers. Diego had been nothing but trouble since the death of his uncle. He hadn't contributed anything to the family, and Jelli was at her end with dealing with him. "I'm not paying that type of money for him, Fate. He's not worth it."

"What? This Cain's nephew we talking about," Fate yelled.

"I don't give a fuck who he is. He's not worth the money or the headache that he is costing this family."

"Well, let's trade the gangsta bitch for him. We got one of theirs and they got one of ours."

"Make it happen then," Jelli said, disappointed that she wasn't going to be killing Racks but she already had her mind up that somebody was going to die about this. Jelli spat on Racks and walked out the room.

Racks overheard the conversation between Jelli and Fate. She laid her head on the concrete and thanked the gangsta God for looking out for her for once.

Jibril Williams

Chapter 27

Daybreak was fast approaching; a thin white line already started to appear in the sky. Whip's phone vibrated again; it was Tata wanting to know what was going on. He sent her call to voicemail; he didn't have time for all the questions that she was going to have. He knew she loved Racks just like she was one of the Red Bottom Squad very own, but she wasn't. Racks was a D.C.B., and she needed his undivided attention. Seeing the pictures that Fate sent of Racks beaten and naked body had him on the verge of losing his mind. He sat in the back seat of the sprinter van. On his lap rested a .40 Glock with a 50-round drum on it. The gun looked like it had a pair of nuts. Boot sat next to him with a mini 14. Pound sat behind the wheel of the sprinter. They sat in the parking lot of Minnesota Ave subway station when Fate revealed that he had Racks and wanted to make a trade for Diego in exchange for Racks. Whip didn't even hesitate to make the exchange. They both agreed that the exchange had to be public, so Minn subway station was agreed upon. But Whip wasn't taking any chances. He had 3 D.C.B.'s posted up across the street, fully loaded and ready for his signal. Diego laid at his feet, duct-taped and bound. He was in bad shape. The van was filled with the sound of him wheezing. Fate hadn't showed up yet. But Whip knew he was close, because the same black GMC had rode past the subway station three times already, and a black Caddy truck had pulled into the parking lot and parked on the other side of it. Phatmama and another of D.C.B. had them covered and ready for a take down if shit popped off.

"Where them pussy ass niggas at?" Boot abruptly said.

185

No one in the sprinter answered his question. All eyes were on the 2020 white Tahoe that just pulled up in the parking lot next to them. The Tahoe had factory tints on them, but silhouettes could be made out in the Tahoe. The Tahoe sat there for about two minutes without anything happening. Whip was on the verge of having his goons move in on the Tahoe, when Boot's burner phone rang.

"Yeah!" he answered.

"I'm ready when you are ready," Fate's voice came through the phone.

"Let's make it happen," Boot said, cutting the call. The back door of the Tahoe opened, and one of Fate's men slid out from the truck cabin, revealing Racks laying on the back seat balled up in a fetal position with a blanket covering her. Jelli sat on the other side of her, holding a gun to her head. Whip slid the sprinter door open. Boot had his timbs on Diego's neck, with the barrel of the mini 14 pressed into the back of Diego's head. The black Caddy truck doors opened, but no one got out. The black GMC truck pulled up a few feet away from the bus stop where D.C.B. was posted up at. Immediately, the air grew tense around them, and the tension between the two groups was off the charts. One false move from either side would cost Minn Ave subway station to erupt in a war.

Whip got out the sprinter and went to grab Racks while Fate's men grabbed Diego off the floor of the sprinter. The two made eye contact, aggressively mugging each other. Fate's goon pulled Diego to his feet. Diego put all his weight on the goon. Whip scooped Racks in his arms; he looked at Jelli with hate. "Don't expect this to be over with."

"I would never rest my head on a pillow and think this would be over. So know that I will be waiting."

Whip didn't respond; he focused his attention on Racks. She felt so feeble in his arms. "I got cha, blood, just hold on, I got cha," Whip whispered, getting back into the sprinter. Boot closed the door. Boot was a strong nigga all the way around the board. All the same, once seeing Racks in her state, he was close to tears. Tears welled up in the corner of his eyes. "Blood, let's get this shit jumping," Boot said, gripping the mini 14 tighter. "Flash your headlights, Pound," Whip said, laying Racks on the back seat. "Blood, they raped me," Racks word barely came over her lips, but Whip could hear her loud and clear.

Pound hit the lights and the D.C.B.'s that were posted at the bus stop started reaching for their weapons. Whip was sliding the sprinter van door back open when a police cruiser pulled up into the parking lot. His lights were flickering red and blue, but there wasn't any sound coming from its sirens. The black caddy doors quickly closed, and the Tahoe immediately pulled out the subway station. The GMC and Caddy truck followed suit. "Damn," Whip stated, easing the van door back close. "Let's roll, Pound!" Whip ordered. Whip picked up his phone. Phatmama picked up on the first ring. "I'm going to pull over once we get over the Benning Road Bridge—Racks going to need medical attention," Whip spoke on the phone. "I need you to take her to the hospital, make up a story about you leaving your house and you found her in your alley. You can tell them what you want just get her to the hospital." Whip disconnected the call and made his way to the back of the sprinter. "Hold on, Racks, we gonna get you some help."

***

"Head straight to the auto shop," Jelli instructed Fate, as she watched her goon cut tape from the mouth and wrist of Diego.

"What! He needs medical attention. Let me get our private doctor on the line."

"Fuck the private doctor, get his ass to the shop. He's a tough guy, he can handle it. That's why he came back to the city when he was supposed to be laying low."

'Come on, Jelli, it's not the time for this shit, we can deal with him later on them issues," Fate said, hitting his turn signal, gearing himself to head in the opposite direction from the auto shop.

"Nigga, if you turn this truck around, I'm gonna turn your brains around," Jelli hissed, pointing her gun at Fate from the back seat. The goon in the back kept his cool and stayed out of the drama. Fate looked at Jelli with hate in his eyes. His thought was that she had lost her mind.

Fate kept this truck on Jelli's demanded designation. The truck's silence was killing Fate. Fifteen minutes later, they had pulled inside the auto body shop. This was the same place she just had Racks rapped at.

Fate pulled the truck into the shop garage and lowered the garage door. Soon as the garage door rested firmly on the ground, Jelli popped two slugs in Diego's head. The gunshots made Fate and his goon draw their weapons. Jelli wiped blood from her face, as she opened the truck door. The gunpowder in the truck started to burn her eyes. Once realization set in as regards what had happened, Fate crawled in the back seat and cradled Diego in his arms. "No, no, no, no, not him, Jelli, why?" Fate asked. Memories of Diego started to flood his mind. He and Cain damn near raised him. Diego was like a real nephew to him, and Cain was like a brother, and he had let both of them down. He wanted to up his banger and empty the clip in Jelli's face, but he knew the Canadian mob would be at his throat. He had to activate his plan. Jelli will definitely pay for this, but he had to know why she did it. "Why? Jelli, why?"

"He's a liability to us, he's wanted by the police for murder and when he got caught by Boot and Whip he started talking. That's how they got your number. Dump the body and burn the truck. I'm heading home to get some rest. This nigga fucked up my shit." Jelli said those words without a care in the world, as she departed the auto shop.

Jibril Williams

Chapter 28

Jelli stomped out the auto shop. She wasn't cool about having to give Racks up for Diego. Fate had begged her to make the swap for Diego, but Fate didn't know she was tired of Diego's shit. Once she'd seen Diego all battered bruised and weeping like a bitch, she'd seen him as weak and knew right then she no longer had room in her organization for him. Fuck if he was Cain's nephew or not, she'd been still feeling the ill vibes from Fate even though he tried his best to conceal them. Jelli knew Fate wasn't going to let ride what she had done to Diego, and she was already prepared for that. She was going to let Weedy have his way with him after she fed his head with some bullshit about Fate. Jelli deactivated the alarm on the G wagon and hopped in. She removed her gun from her hip and placed it under her right leg. Then she removed some exotic bag called *White Widow*. She twisted a fat one and sparked the exotic up. Jelli hit the power button on the thick system and Jhene Aiko's *Blue Dreams* came blaring through the truck speakers. Jelli hit the marijuana, and eased her whip away from the curb. The morning traffic was picking up, and the city of D.C. was woken. The residents were headed to work, and the night shift workers were heading home. Jelli couldn't wait to get home herself; she was tired as fuck. And she felt gritty from being out all night. She reflected on her night, and it was crazy to her how she went from partying to almost having to shoot her way out club Red Bottomz with Tata, to having Racks make an attempt on her life, to having to kill Diego. *I'm living a helluva life*, Jelli thought to herself. Her life made her feel powerful and untouchable. A red light had Jelli held up. She puffed viciously on her weed. The exotic had her buzzing good; her eyes were low, but she was aware of her surroundings. She cracked her window, letting a cloud of smoke escape the truck's cabin. The light turned green. Jelli hit the gas, pushing the Benz through the light, losing grip on the weed; it fell in her lap, burning a hole in her pants instantly. Jelli felt the heat of the spliffy in her skin, causing her to jerk the wheel slightly before she could retrieve the burning weed from her lap. "Shit!" Jelli yelled, placing the spliffy between her lips and knocking ashes off her lap. She removed the gun from under her, and placed it on the passenger seat, putting her eye back on the road and then back down at her damaged pants.

Jelli was mad that she had ruined her pink pants. When Jelli brought her eyes back up to the road, she was caught off guard and sighted the red and blue lights flashing in her rearview. "Fuck!" Jelli yelled, putting the weed out and trying to rid the truck of smoke. Jelli drove a few blocks before she pulled over. She got all her info out her hand nearby that she would need, and placed the gun between the seats. A tall black officer got out of his cruiser and walked towards Jelli's truck. He wore dark shades, so it was hard to read his eyes. Jelli rolled her window down.

"License, registration, and proof of insurance?" the officer asked with a no-bullshit tone. Without even saying, "Good morning, ma'am." Jelli knew right then this muthafucka was going to be a jerk.

"Good morning to you, officer," Jelli said, handing him her license and other requested info.

"Sit tight, I will be right back," the officer said, walking back towards his car. Jelli knew he was getting ready to run her name through the system. Jelli dialed Fate's number, but it went straight to voicemail. She tried it again—same result. "Fuck!" she mumbled. The officer had Jelli waiting a good twenty minutes before he came back to her truck.

"Ms. Angellia Roberts, could you please step out of your vehicle?" the officer asked with his hand resting on the butt of his gun. Jelli looked confused, but she complied with the officer's request. She finally paid attention to the officer's name tag, and learned that his name was Powell.

"What's the problem, Officer Powell?"

"The problem is that I've seen you drifting side to side in traffic and when I approached your truck I could smell marijuana."

"Weed could be smoked for recreational purposes in DC," Jelli said in her defense.

"Yeah, it is, but not if you're in federal probation. You are on supervised release, right?" Officer Powell asked. The lump in Jelli's throat was so big she could hardly swallow.

"Yes, sir, I'm on supervised release," Jelli said with a little attitude.

"Ms. Roberts, please place your hands behind your back."

Jelli couldn't believe what she was hearing.

"Hands behind my back for what! A little bit of weed?"

"Ma'am, place your hand behind your back, don't let me tell you again," Officer Powell stated more firmly. Jelli hesitated, but she came into compliance. Officer Powell placed cuffs on Jelli's tiny wrist and escorted her back to the front of his cruiser.

"I'm going to search your car and if it's clean, then I will let you go. Is there anything else in your truck besides marijuana?"

"No," Jelli mumbled.

Officer Powell approached Jelli's truck. He looked back at Jelli before he opened the driver side door. Jelli stared back at him with the puppy look. He opened the truck door, and started his search and it wasn't long before he withdrew from Jelli's truck, holding up a smoke-gray Ruger in the air. Jelli had forgotten all about the gun. She started hyperventilating before she passed out.

***

The whole Red Bottom Squad was at Washington Hospital center. Tata and Billie met Phatmama at the hospital once she got the call from Whip informing her about what happened to Racks. Tata paced back and forth in the waiting room. Billie played the corner of the waiting room, trying to get comfortable in a hard orange plastic chair. Phatmama stared off in space; Tata could just imagine what was going on in her head. Racks was rushed into surgery. The doctors stated that her rectum was ripped badly, and one of her lungs had collapsed. The group had been waiting over two hours. Tata was plotting on her next move with Jelli. The bitch had to get hers. Tata was feeling bad that Racks was hurt by the hands of Jelli. Her thought went back to the convo they had at the car dealership. Tata felt like she had let Racks down. Most of all, she had let Zoey down. A short Asian woman walked into the waiting room, wearing pink scrubs and white doctor's lab coat on top of them. "Family of Rita Young?" she called out.

"Yes, that's us," Phatmama yelled out. She jumped up and approached the doc. Tata and Billie joined her.

"I'm Doctor Sue. I performed surgery on Rita Young."

"Is she going to be okay?" Phatmama asked.

The doctor let out a long sigh.

"She's going to be fine. She just needs a lot of rest. We had to give a temporary colostomy bag because of the damage done to her rectum.

"When can we see her?" Tata asked.

"I'm going to recommend no visit until twenty-four hours and the police talk to Ms. Young. It's our policy that all gunshot and rape victims have to be reported to the police." Just then, the doctor was paged over the loudspeaker. "Well, if that's all, I have to go," Doctor Sue said, before walking out the waiting room.

"Since we know that she is going to be okay, let's go home and get some rest and we will come back tomorrow," Phatmama said. She felt like she needed a shower and to be up under Boot's hard body.

Jibril Williams

Chapter 29

16 days later

Racks exhaled a deep sigh. It had been two weeks and two days since she was brutally raped. Even though her body was recovering and healing with every day she spent in the hospital, her emotions and mental state were withering away. For days as she lay in the hospital bed, she contemplated suicide. She didn't have the desire to live anymore or to seek revenge against those who violated her. Racks looked around the small hospital room that was flooded with cards, balloons and flowers wishing her a speedy recovery. But none of that mattered to her because she would never recover. She would never bounce back from her situation. Tears welled up in her eyes; she fought hard to stop them by wiping them away with her hand, but the effort was frivolous because the tears seemed to pour down in torrents. Snot oozed from her nose, and she snorted it back into her nostrils. Racks couldn't believe how dramatically her life had unfolded. She couldn't believe her endgame was what it was. D.C.B. and the Red Bottom Squad had been flooding her with visits and love; that's how her room got filled with all the get-well paraphernalia. Even though she'd seen her people daily, she still could not utter what was going on with her. Racks balled her hands into fists, clenched her teeth and screamed. She wanted to lash out at something or someone, but there was no one there. She whipped her tears away with the back of her hands. She was scheduled for discharge at 12:00 p.m. Whip was going to come pick her up along with Tata. She had about an hour before they got there. Racks eased herself out the hospital bed and stood to her feet. Pain immediately rung out from her rectum. Her sphincter muscle was ripped in the process of the rape that led Rack to have nine stiches in her rectum, and a colostomy bag. The soreness in her ass made her take baby steps towards the bathroom. What would have been a few seconds walk took Racks a whole two minutes to get to the bathroom. She lifted her gown and slowly squatted in the toilet to pee.

***

"Boot! Bae, you too deep! Oh, bae, my stomach!" Phatmama cried out as she clinched the bed sheets in her fist. Boot had Phatmama's legs dropped over his shoulders, stroking his glistening black rod into her buttery hole. Ever since Boot had proposed to Phatmama she'd been giving the pussy up on demand like Netflix. Their first encounter was rough for Boot because it was like Phatmama was a virgin all over again. He had to take his time inserting his manhood and after all of that, Boot learned that Phatmama was just like most chubby thick girls. She couldn't take no dick. Instead of gutting her out with no regard, like most niggas would have done when they came across a chick that couldn't take the D, Boot took his time with Phatmama and slow-stroked like he was doing now. Boot pulled out to his tip, and pushed back into Phatmama's gushiness all the way to his hilt, resting his nuts against her brown hole. He would hold this position and then stir his manhood in a circle motion in Phatmama's goodies. You could hear the wet smacking sound like you heard when your grandma put mayo in the bowl to whip to potato salad. Boot pulled out to the head and repeated his dick motion down. Phatmama's legs trembled over Boot's shoulders during the whole process. She came so many times she lost count. Phatmama had become madly in love with Boot hands down. Boot was her king.

He never made her feel inadequate, and she adored that about him. Boot allowed her to be her. He accepted her and her savage ways. Phatmama shook hard again.

"Boot, Boot, baby, if—if—I cum one more time, I'm gonna faint," Phatmama whispered. Boot didn't verbally respond. He was holding off on his orgasm, wanting to please his woman and helping Phatmama get used to his length. He didn't care what a nigga said, pussy was way better then fucking a chick in the dookie chute. Boot increased the pace of his strokes. "Oh baby—oh baby—I'm telling you! You—" Phatmama groaned as her eyes rolled in the back of her head in pleasure of Boot's thrusts. Boot felt the pressure in his sack building up, and he couldn't partake in Phatmama's love box any longer. He released his load deep in her tunnel. Boot released Phatmama's legs from over his shoulders. He fell between her legs with his meat still in her. Phatmama wrapped her thick legs around Boot's body, locking him into place. He could still feel the walls of her pussy constrict and jerk around his pipe.

"I love you, Boot," Phatmama said passionately.

"I love you too, Phat," Boot reciprocated Phatmama's love, and placed a wet kiss on her lips. Phatmama stared in Boot's eyes, and a feeling washed over her while Boot still had wood in her; it felt like her and Boot's heart was connected, like their hearts were beating in sync to the same rhythm. At that moment, Phatmama felt the truest form of love that she ever experienced in her life. A look of understanding appeared in Boot's eyes, and right then and there Phatmama knew Boot was feeling what she was feeling. It dawned on her that what's understood doesn't need to be said. This was one of those things that soul mates do communicate without words. The moment would forever be embedded in both of their memories.

"You hungry, Phat?" Boot asked, removing himself from the confinements of Phatmama's legs.

"Yup! A chick could use some grub." Phatmama got out of bed, and pulled a red t-shirt over her head that had the words *Boot chic* plastered on the front of it in bold black letters. A gift Boot gave to her. This was what she slept in and wore around Boot's crib when she stayed the night. "You going to cook something or we going to hit up a spot?" Boot asked, as he started rolling some bud packs in a Vega.

"Well, let's take a quick shower and go grab some brunch since it's so late in the day. Then you can drop me off over Tata's house. I want to be there when Whip and Tata bring Racks home from the hospital." Phatmama took the freshly rolled Vega from Boot's hand, lighting it with the Bic lighter she retrieved off the dresser. She took three long pulls, handed it back to Boot, and headed towards the bathroom to start her shower. Boot sat on the bed and took pull after pull of the Vega; this was his first smoke of the day. He needed to get his mind right. He had a lot of shit to do dealing with D.C.B. business. The traps needed to be checked on, then him and Sticks had to meet up with the nigga Flame to see what's good with the info he got on Jelli. Thinking of Jelli made him think of Racks and how Jelli's men fucked her over. He knew the lil' homie was going to run the murder rate up for that shit that happened to her. Rose—Boot's red-nose pitbull—came trolling into the room she put her head between Boot legs. He rubbed her big head. "What's up, girl? You need to go outside or you need a hit?" Boot asked Rose like he was talking with a real person, and as if she knew every word that was being said to her. Rose stood on her hind legs, and rested her front paws in Boot's thigh. Boot chuckled as he flipped the Vega around and blew a shotgun. It was crazy how he watched the dog inhale the smoke. This was something he had been doing with Rose since she was a pup.

"Boot, come on and get in the shower with me so we can get outta here!" Phatmama yelled from the bathroom.

"Alright, let me let Rose out in the backyard so she can handle her business," Boot replied. "Come on, girl, let's go." Boot started downstairs with Rose behind him. Boot entered the kitchen and stepped out the back door. Rose started to growl. "What the fuck you got going on, girl? Let me find out you tripping." Boot peeked out the back door window; staring back at him were three figures on his back porch, wearing masks. Boot sprinted on his heels, trying to make it upstairs. Halfway up the stairs, he could hear the back door being kicked in—as well as the front door.

Boom-Boom! Gun shots could be heard coming from the kitchen, and Rose barking. Phatmama heard all the commotion, and met Boot as she came out the bathroom dripping wet with fear in her eyes.

"It's a hit, Phat!" Boot ran, pushed her and flipped the mattress on the bed, and snatched up the chopper. Phatmama grabbed the chrome pump. Boot stepped back into the hallway, spitting the choppa. Men in all-black were rushing up the steps. Boot sent helluva bullets their way. Phatmama stood beside him, naked, emptying out her pump. It was then she realized that it was the police they were shooting at.

The police returned fire, grazing Phatmama in the thigh, but Boot wasn't so lucky. Shots after shots entered and ripped flesh from his body; holes after holes appeared in his chest. Boot stumbled and fell to his back.

"Nooooo! Nooooo! Baby, please hold on, please, baby, hold—" Phatmama dropped to her knees and cradled Boot's head in her arms. "Hold on, baby, I'm going to get you some help," Phatmama said, crying. She yelled over her shoulder, calling out to the police that held court at the bottom of the stairs: "We give up! Please don't shoot no more. He's been hurt bad!"

"Throw your weapon down the stairs," an officer said. Phatmama quickly complied with the officer's demands by throwing the choppa and pump down the stairs.

"Now come get him—He is bleeding out up here," Phatmama screamed. She went back to Boot's aid. "Keep them beautiful eyes open, baby. We gonna pull through this—" Phat continued to talk to a bleeding out Boot. Blood was leaking from everywhere on Boot's body. He struggled to breathe and when he finally did, dark blood erupted from his mouth. Phatmama knew from combat in Afghanistan: when this happened, a person was in bad shape. She panicked even further. "He needs help, he is dying. Please help."

Boot closed his eyes, then immediately opened them. You could tell he was struggling hard to focus. "Phat, with all my heart I love you—You would for—forever be my—my wife. Tell my nigga Whip to keep it *suu-wuu.*" Boot locked eyes with his savage queen, as life slowly drained from his eyes.

Phatmama held Boot's head in her lap and arms, and rocked back and forth. She leaned over and kissed Boot's bloody lips. "I love you, baby," Phatmama whispered, as she closed Boot's lifeless eyes.

Chapter 30

Racks finally made it out the bathroom. After using it, washing her face and brushing her teeth, it took her awhile to put her clothes on, but she managed just fine. She made it back to her bed where she pushed her feet into a pair of black and red J's. Racks was ready to go home to a familiar place and get away from all the people that wanted to probe her, take her vitals, and give her advice about how she could manage through her condition. Most importantly, she was tired of the police coming up to the hospital every other day asking the same old questions about who raped her, or whether she could remember anything about her attackers. No matter how much Racks showered, she could never overcome the thought of feeling dirty. She needed something to numb her and erase the image of Jelli's men raping her. And the only thing that could help her with that was an ounce of that potent Cali bud, and a fifth of Cîroc. She already anticipated indulging in the two once she made it home. Tata and Whip had plans for her to shack up with them until she got better, but she had a change of plans. She wanted to be alone with her thoughts and misery. Racks looked at her watch and saw that it was 11:21a.m. Whip and Tata would be there shortly. She eased herself back into the bed and tried to be comfortable. Nurse Pihl entered the room without saying anything to her; she avoided eye contact with Racks. The nurse went to her duties in terms of checking Racks' vitals one last time before she was to be released.

"Are my discharge papers ready and have my friends got here to pick me up yet?" Rack asked, watching the nurse closely.

Nurse Pihl was beautiful, mixed with black and white descent. She was in her forties. Since Racks had been admitted to the hospital, the nurse had always been very pleasant and talkative with Racks. But today nurse Pihl was off. "Yes, your discharge papers—I will get them in a minute—I'm checking your vitals so you could be released," Nurse Pihl said, without making eye contact. "And there is someone here to pick you up—I would be right back with your discharge papers and prescription for your meds," Ms. Pihl said, quickly leaving the room. Racks sat there, feeling weird from nurse Pihl's actions. She wondered if it was because nurse Pihl felt indifferent about her sickness. That's why she already made up her mind not to tell anyone about her condition. It would kill her if Whip ever treated her differently because of her status.

Nurse Pihl came back into the room moments later with her discharge papers. Racks quickly signed them. "Could you please tell whoever's here to pick me up I'm ready?" Rack said, getting out of bed. Nurse Pihl looked at Racks for the first time and whispered. "I'm sorry."

Racks' face crinkled up in confusion. "Sorry for what?" Racks asked. Nurse Pihl didn't reply; she just exited the room. Shortly after, two police officers entered her room. Racks became instantaneously irritated. "Like I told the other police officers, I don't know who raped me," Racks said with her face balled up.

"We're not here about your rape. We wish they would have killed your ass. We're here to arrest you for the murder of metropolitan police officer McClain." Racks became light-headed, and she fell to her knees.

***

"I want to use whatever info we can get from Flame—I want to apply some pressure on her, Whip," Tata said from behind the wheel of her Ferrari truck. Whip sat low in the passenger seat, blowing sour diesel.

"I'm on it, baby, I just want to make sure we can trust this nigga Flame. I sent word to the big homies out west, and word came down that he's official and about his paper and his gun game is impeccable."

"Well, all that shit is good to know but let's start putting some shit in play because Jelli has become a vicious thorn in my side! I'm not going to let Racks' situation go unchecked." Tata felt fuck up about getting raped. Her thought reflected back to the convo her and Racks had at the car dealership. Racks wanted to smash the gas on Jelli, but she wanted to slow-walk the bed and get money. Now Racks was lying in the hospital from being raped by Jelli's men. Tata shook her head at the thought.

Blowing smoke out his nose, Whip spoke: "We gonna handle shit, babe, you don't even have to worry about that. I put my G on that shit. He paused, then changed the subject. You heard about them finding ol' boy's body in an alley on Newton St?" He didn't want to talk about Racks.

"Who?"

"That nigga Diego," Whip replied nonchalantly.

"Damn!" That was all Tata muttered before her and Whip's phones started ringing. Tata saw it was Rau'f; she sent it to voicemail. She was on her way to grab Racks from the hospital; she would call him once she got Racks settled in. They were just pulling up to the hospital. Whip answered his phone; immediately, his face frowned up. He flipped his phone around in his hand and activated the Fox news app on his phone. His screen captured the front of Boot's house. Police led Phatmama out the house in handcuffs with a bed sheet wrapped around her. She had evidence of blood on her face. Her head was hung low. Moments later, the police brought out a body bag from the house. The news lady began to narrate the events:

"This morning, sometime around, 11 a.m., police approached the house behind us to serve a no-knock warrant. The warrant was for Tanya Foxx. Upon officers breaching the house, officers were met with gunfire from some type of assault rifle. Several officers were wounded. One officer was pronounced dead at the scene. The shooter—Terrance "Boot" Dixium—was shot by officers and died on the scene as well. Tanya Foxx is now being led into custody. It is alleged that she is the *Genital Killer*. Authorities say her fingerprints were discovered at one of her victims' crime scene. Also, authorities were tipped off that Tanya "Phatmama" Foxx is a member of the all-women jewelry store robbers that have all the jewelry merchants shoot up."

Tata's phone vibrated again; it was Rau'f. She ignored the call.

Whip turned his phone off. He removed the bifocals from his face, and wiped the fresh tears from his face.

Tata couldn't find the words to console Whip. She just wrapped her arms around his neck, as he cried like a baby for the loss of his childhood friend. Tata never heard a man holler the way Whip did into the crook of her neck. Her own tears started to fall from her eyes. Tata's phone vibrated again. Knowing shit was falling apart, she knew she needed to answer the call. "Hello," Tata answered, pulling herself away from Whip, and placing the phone on speaker.

"Tata, this is Rau'f. My people just informed me that you are in great danger. They are raiding the club. You are wanted for everything from robbing to murder. My plane is leaving for Morocco in one hour. You need to be on it. I'm texting you the info now." Rau'f didn't give Tata a chance to reply. If she wanted to, she couldn't because her words were caught in her throat as she watched two police officers roll Racks out in a wheelchair bound in handcuffs.

To Be Continued...
The Heart of a Savage 4
Coming Soon

Submission Guideline

Submit the first three chapters of your completed manuscript to ldpsubmissions@gmail.com, subject line: Your book's title. The manuscript must be in a .doc file and sent as an attachment. Document should be in Times New Roman, double spaced and in size 12 font. Also, provide your synopsis and full contact information. If sending multiple submissions, they must each be in a separate email.

Have a story but no way to send it electronically? You can still submit to LDP/Ca$h Presents. Send in the first three chapters, written or typed, of your completed manuscript to:

LDP: Submissions Dept
Po Box 944
Stockbridge, Ga 30281

DO NOT send original manuscript. Must be a duplicate.

Provide your synopsis and a cover letter containing your full contact information.

Thanks for considering LDP and Ca$h Presents.

Coming Soon from Lock Down Publications/Ca$h Presents

BOW DOWN TO MY GANGSTA

By Ca$h

TORN BETWEEN TWO

By Coffee

THE STREETS STAINED MY SOUL **II**

By Marcellus Allen

BLOOD OF A BOSS **VI**

SHADOWS OF THE GAME II

TRAP BASTARD II

By Askari

LOYAL TO THE GAME **IV**

By T.J. & Jelissa

IF LOVING YOU IS WRONG… **III**

By Jelissa

TRUE SAVAGE **VIII**

MIDNIGHT CARTEL IV

DOPE BOY MAGIC IV

CITY OF KINGZ III

By Chris Green

BLAST FOR ME **III**

A SAVAGE DOPEBOY III

CUTTHROAT MAFIA III

DUFFLE BAG CARTEL VI

Jibril Williams

HEARTLESS GOON VI
By Ghost
KILL ZONE **II**
BAE BELONGS TO ME III
A DOPE BOY'S QUEEN III
By Aryanna
COKE KINGS V
KING OF THE TRAP II
By T.J. Edwards
GORILLAZ IN THE BAY V
3X KRAZY III
By De'Kari
THE STREETS ARE CALLING II
By Duquie Wilson
KINGPIN KILLAZ IV
STREET KINGS III
PAID IN BLOOD III
CARTEL KILLAZ IV
DOPE GODS III
By Hood Rich
SINS OF A HUSTLA II
By ASAD
KINGZ OF THE GAME VI
By Playa Ray
SLAUGHTER GANG IV
RUTHLESS HEART IV

By Willie Slaughter

FUK SHYT II

By Blakk Diamond

TRAP QUEEN

By Troublesome

YAYO V

By S. Allen

GHOST MOB II

By Stilloan Robinson

KINGPIN DREAMS III

By Paper Boi Rari

CREAM II

By Yolanda Moore

SON OF A DOPE FIEND III

By Renta

FOREVER GANGSTA II

GLOCKS ON SATIN SHEETS III

By Adrian Dulan

LOYALTY AIN'T PROMISED III

By Keith Williams

THE PRICE YOU PAY FOR LOVE III

By Destiny Skai

I'M NOTHING WITHOUT HIS LOVE II

SINS OF A THUG II

By Monet Dragun

LIFE OF A SAVAGE IV

MURDA SEASON IV

GANGLAND CARTEL IV

CHI'RAQ GANGSTAS III

By Romell Tukes

QUIET MONEY IV

EXTENDED CLIP III

By Trai'Quan

THE STREETS MADE ME III

By Larry D. Wright

IF YOU CROSS ME ONCE II

ANGEL III

By Anthony Fields

FRIEND OR FOE III

By Mimi

SAVAGE STORMS III

By Meesha

BLOOD ON THE MONEY III

By J-Blunt

THE STREETS WILL NEVER CLOSE II

By K'ajji

NIGHTMARES OF A HUSTLA III

By King Dream

THE WIFEY I USED TO BE II

By Nicole Goosby

IN THE ARM OF HIS BOSS

By Jamila

MONEY, MURDER & MEMORIES III

By Malik D. Rice

CONCRETE KILLAZ II

By Kingpen

HARD AND RUTHLESS II

By Von Wiley Hall

LEVELS TO THIS SHYT II

By Ah'Million

MOB TIES II

By SayNoMore

BODYMORE MURDERLAND II

By Delmont Player

THE LAST OF THE OGS II

By Tranay Adams

Jibril Williams

Available Now

RESTRAINING ORDER **I & II**
By CA$H & Coffee
LOVE KNOWS NO BOUNDARIES **I II & III**
By Coffee
RAISED AS A GOON I, II, III & IV
BRED BY THE SLUMS I, II, III
BLAST FOR ME I & II
ROTTEN TO THE CORE I II III
A BRONX TALE I, II, III
DUFFLE BAG CARTEL I II III IV V
HEARTLESS GOON I II III IV V
A SAVAGE DOPEBOY I II
DRUG LORDS I II III
CUTTHROAT MAFIA I II
By Ghost
LAY IT DOWN **I & II**
LAST OF A DYING BREED I II
BLOOD STAINS OF A SHOTTA I & II III
By Jamaica
LOYAL TO THE GAME I II III
LIFE OF SIN I, II III
By TJ & Jelissa
BLOODY COMMAS I & II

SKI MASK CARTEL I II & III

KING OF NEW YORK I II,III IV V

RISE TO POWER I II III

COKE KINGS I II III IV

BORN HEARTLESS I II III IV

KING OF THE TRAP

By T.J. Edwards

IF LOVING HIM IS WRONG…I & II

LOVE ME EVEN WHEN IT HURTS I II III

By Jelissa

WHEN THE STREETS CLAP BACK I & II III

THE HEART OF A SAVAGE I II III

By Jibril Williams

A DISTINGUISHED THUG STOLE MY HEART I II & III

LOVE SHOULDN'T HURT I II III IV

RENEGADE BOYS I II III IV

PAID IN KARMA I II III

SAVAGE STORMS I II

By Meesha

A GANGSTER'S CODE I &, II III

A GANGSTER'S SYN I II III

THE SAVAGE LIFE I II III

CHAINED TO THE STREETS I II III

BLOOD ON THE MONEY I II

By J-Blunt

PUSH IT TO THE LIMIT

Jibril Williams

By Bre' Hayes

BLOOD OF A BOSS **I, II, III, IV, V**

SHADOWS OF THE GAME

TRAP BASTARD

By Askari

THE STREETS BLEED MURDER **I, II & III**

THE HEART OF A GANGSTA I II& III

By Jerry Jackson

CUM FOR ME I II III IV V VI

An LDP Erotica Collaboration

BRIDE OF A HUSTLA **I II & II**

THE FETTI GIRLS **I, II& III**

CORRUPTED BY A GANGSTA I, II III, IV

BLINDED BY HIS LOVE

THE PRICE YOU PAY FOR LOVE I II

DOPE GIRL MAGIC I II III

By Destiny Skai

WHEN A GOOD GIRL GOES BAD

By Adrienne

THE COST OF LOYALTY I II III

By Kweli

A GANGSTER'S REVENGE **I II III & IV**

THE BOSS MAN'S DAUGHTERS I II III IV V

A SAVAGE LOVE **I & II**

BAE BELONGS TO ME I II

A HUSTLER'S DECEIT I, II, III

216

WHAT BAD BITCHES DO I, II, III

SOUL OF A MONSTER I II III

KILL ZONE

A DOPE BOY'S QUEEN I II

By Aryanna

A KINGPIN'S AMBITON

A KINGPIN'S AMBITION **II**

I MURDER FOR THE DOUGH

By Ambitious

TRUE SAVAGE I II III IV V VI VII

DOPE BOY MAGIC I, II, III

MIDNIGHT CARTEL I II III

CITY OF KINGZ I II

By Chris Green

A DOPEBOY'S PRAYER

By Eddie "Wolf" Lee

THE KING CARTEL **I, II & III**

By Frank Gresham

THESE NIGGAS AIN'T LOYAL **I, II & III**

By Nikki Tee

GANGSTA SHYT **I II &III**

By CATO

THE ULTIMATE BETRAYAL

By Phoenix

BOSS'N UP **I , II & III**

By Royal Nicole

Jibril Williams

I LOVE YOU TO DEATH
By Destiny J
I RIDE FOR MY HITTA
I STILL RIDE FOR MY HITTA
By Misty Holt
LOVE & CHASIN' PAPER
By Qay Crockett
TO DIE IN VAIN
SINS OF A HUSTLA
By ASAD
BROOKLYN HUSTLAZ
By Boogsy Morina
BROOKLYN ON LOCK I & II
By Sonovia
GANGSTA CITY
By Teddy Duke
A DRUG KING AND HIS DIAMOND I & II III
A DOPEMAN'S RICHES
HER MAN, MINE'S TOO I, II
CASH MONEY HO'S
THE WIFEY I USED TO BE
By Nicole Goosby
TRAPHOUSE KING **I II & III**
KINGPIN KILLAZ I II III
STREET KINGS I II
PAID IN BLOOD **I II**

218

CARTEL KILLAZ I II III

DOPE GODS I II

By Hood Rich

LIPSTICK KILLAH **I, II, III**

CRIME OF PASSION I II & III

FRIEND OR FOE I II

By Mimi

STEADY MOBBN' **I, II, III**

THE STREETS STAINED MY SOUL

By Marcellus Allen

WHO SHOT YA **I, II, III**

SON OF A DOPE FIEND I II

By Renta

GORILLAZ IN THE BAY **I II III IV**

TEARS OF A GANGSTA I II

3X KRAZY I II

By DE'KARI

TRIGGADALE I II III

By Elijah R. Freeman

GOD BLESS THE TRAPPERS I, II, III

THESE SCANDALOUS STREETS I, II, III

FEAR MY GANGSTA I, II, III IV, V

THESE STREETS DON'T LOVE NOBODY I, II

BURY ME A G I, II, III, IV, V

A GANGSTA'S EMPIRE I, II, III, IV

THE DOPEMAN'S BODYGAURD I II

Jibril Williams

THE REALEST KILLAZ I II III

THE LAST OF THE OGS

By Tranay Adams

THE STREETS ARE CALLING

By Duquie Wilson

MARRIED TO A BOSS... I II III

By Destiny Skai & Chris Green

KINGZ OF THE GAME I II III IV V

By Playa Ray

SLAUGHTER GANG I II III

RUTHLESS HEART I II III

By Willie Slaughter

FUK SHYT

By Blakk Diamond

DON'T F#CK WITH MY HEART I II

By Linnea

ADDICTED TO THE DRAMA I II III

IN THE ARM OF HIS BOSS II

By Jamila

YAYO I II III IV

A SHOOTER'S AMBITION I II

By S. Allen

TRAP GOD I II III

By Troublesome

FOREVER GANGSTA

GLOCKS ON SATIN SHEETS I II

By Adrian Dulan

TOE TAGZ I II III

LEVELS TO THIS SHYT

By Ah'Million

KINGPIN DREAMS I II

By Paper Boi Rari

CONFESSIONS OF A GANGSTA I II III

By Nicholas Lock

I'M NOTHING WITHOUT HIS LOVE

SINS OF A THUG

By Monet Dragun

CAUGHT UP IN THE LIFE I II III

By Robert Baptiste

NEW TO THE GAME I II III

MONEY, MURDER & MEMORIES I II

By Malik D. Rice

LIFE OF A SAVAGE I II III

A GANGSTA'S QUR'AN I II III

MURDA SEASON I II III

GANGLAND CARTEL I II III

CHI'RAQ GANGSTAS I II

By Romell Tukes

LOYALTY AIN'T PROMISED I II

By Keith Williams

QUIET MONEY I II III

THUG LIFE I II

Jibril Williams

EXTENDED CLIP I II
By **Trai'Quan**
THE STREETS MADE ME I II
By Larry D. Wright
THE ULTIMATE SACRIFICE I, II, III, IV, V, VI
KHADIFI
IF YOU CROSS ME ONCE
ANGEL I II
By Anthony Fields
THE LIFE OF A HOOD STAR
By Ca$h & Rashia Wilson
THE STREETS WILL NEVER CLOSE
By K'ajji
CREAM
By Yolanda Moore
NIGHTMARES OF A HUSTLA I II
By King Dream
CONCRETE KILLAZ
By Kingpen
HARD AND RUTHLESS
By Von Wiley Hall
GHOST MOB II
By Stilloan Robinson
MOB TIES
By SayNoMore
BODYMORE MURDERLAND

By Delmont Player

FOR THE LOVE OF A BOSS

By C. D. Blue

Jibril Williams

<u>BOOKS BY LDP'S CEO, CA$H</u>

<u>TRUST IN NO MAN</u>

<u>TRUST IN NO MAN 2</u>

<u>TRUST IN NO MAN 3</u>

<u>BONDED BY BLOOD</u>

<u>SHORTY GOT A THUG</u>

<u>THUGS CRY</u>

<u>THUGS CRY 2</u>

<u>THUGS CRY 3</u>

<u>TRUST NO BITCH</u>

<u>TRUST NO BITCH 2</u>

<u>TRUST NO BITCH 3</u>

<u>TIL MY CASKET DROPS</u>

<u>RESTRAINING ORDER</u>

<u>RESTRAINING ORDER 2</u>

<u>IN LOVE WITH A CONVICT</u>

<u>LIFE OF A HOOD STAR</u>

The Heart of a Savage 3